i

future

Serpent Dove

Elder Adok

Published by Hiss Farm Concepts

In a generation or two
England could be like this.
Serpent Dove teases strands
of wisdom, choice, power
and love in such an age.

Here's to those
who will inherit this earth.

Thanks

Having failed English 'O level' twice I am indebted to Moll Flanders for my interest in literature, and to Ray Bradbury for his world 'brilliant with information'.

I am grateful to a number of people whose contributions they wish to keep anonymous.

It is a pleasure to acknowledge Alex, folk music enthusiast, for proof reading; Ali, psychotherapist, on bees and value indices; Beryl, grandmother, on character; Betty, retired teacher, on theme; Brenda, retired teacher, on style and for proof reading; Brian, sailor, on animal intelligence; Charles, doctor, on storyline; Courtenay, sportswoman, on integrated vision; Deirdre, author, on style; Geoffrey, farmer, on morality; Graeme, anaesthetist, on environment; Jean, retired social worker, on the wisdom of elders; John, guitarist, for proof reading; Kim, volunteer, on emotion and for proof reading; Kimberley, teacher, on technology and storyline; Kirsty, teaching assistant, for her typing, proof reading, and insight into colour; Lewis, engineer, on regenerative genes; Polly, novelist, on drama; Ronald, physician, on morality; Thomas, lawyer, on storyline; and Air Training Corps Cadets on themes.

My thanks to NASA for their image of the moon Io.

Where's where

1 ~ Serpent Dove

2 ~ Loose Ends

Who's Who

Freeman brothers	Basil [31 years, 'emotionally' 11] George [25, security operative]

Metaguild	Gustav Kimmler [27, history tutor]
	Pete Roberts [40, chaplain]
	    Alfred Cookson [18, student]
	    Ashley Woodlander [16, student]
	    Pamela Smith [16, student]
	    William Inchbald [16, student]
	    Zoid Shevardnadze [17, student]

Silvanus' Cell	Montague Woodlander [65, pilot] Jeanette Pack [31, PR services] Charles Jarman [39, analyst] Victor Ford [34, computer boffin]

Smith
family
	Robert [99, aka Greatpa]
	= Louise [95, aka Greatma]
	    Siman [75, aka Grandpa]
	    = Janu [76, aka Granny Smith]
	        Arthor [56, telecoms architect]
	        = Claru [55, administrator]
	            Io [25, programmer]

Woodlander
family
	Montague [65, pilot]
	= Cynthia [50, tea lady]
	    Silvanus [33, rider maintenance]
	    = Holly [34, hairdresser]
	        Ashley [16, student]
	    (= Jeanette [26, PR services])
	        Fern & Ernest [2, twins]

| Others | Tweedy [52, security analyst] |
| | Ivana Spicer [45, politician] |

What's What

beach	portal to the swell
bronchs	cycle and fresh air ways
buddy	body umbilical for data and diary, usually fitted into a shoe
ESP	Even Space Protocol for rider positioning
Inflow	Information flow control complex, aka The Fish
metaguild	education for 16+ scholars
pic	personal identity chip in wrist bone
rider	telecoms station riding in stratosphere
sab	combined sphinx and buddy
sphinx	United Nations standard personal hook into network 'x'; *'voice' shown by italics*
swell	UN internet available equally to all
V2L	'Value to Living' index

Elder Adok's bio

Elder Adok's childhood
was spent in Africa before attending
boarding schools in the south of England.
His work in both industrial and voluntary sectors
has given him widespread knowledge of
and remarkable insight into the
potential of his fellow man.

His realistic but unjaded
passion for life and the world around him
takes his readers on journeys that not
only let them see his thoughts
but inspires their own.

Dedication

To fresh air

01 Questioning

Nature could not have made her more perfect. As Io plunged naked into the cool water it was as if innocence had broken through a shimmering mirror. Her only blemish was the pic mark made at birth, yet personal identity chips were far more convenient than those old fashioned smart cards and funny bits of paper. She was a child of her age and had 110 years to live anywhere in the world.

Io relished this freedom, this adventure. Fair hair at birth colluded with a trend of the day so that her parents named her Io after a bright moon circulating around Jupiter. The scene looked innocent too, for the pool was illuminated by tropical moonlight. It was almost as if Io the planet caressed Io the damsel. But as she swam she was reflecting. Aged twenty five, this was no mid-life crisis, rather it was a rising unease with her amazing beaching skills. Unease had been detected and Io was being watched.

Somehow the space and beauty of the tropics spoke to the very soul of this comely maiden. Io had poise. Her body was pleasingly balanced, perfectly proportioned. If she were speaking to the loins of a male she could yield immense power. As George watched her gracefully emerge from the pool he found reason faltered under the bidding of such an apparition. Yet George had to monitor Io not get involved with her. Objectivity was the first call in surveillance. He had state of the art devices at his disposal so that Io would be unaware of his sight and hearing. She was however no fool, and knew the power of her beauty. She knew too that she was being observed. Mentally she had detected George some time ago even though they had never met. She was not frightened; in fact he might be able to quell her unease. How did she know it was a man who watched?

The Inflow complex was by design both security conscious and breath-taking. It was awesome in its domination of the Fens and could be seen from eighty kilometres away. Rarely had an information organism centred on silicon technology blended so well with the natural world based on the carbon chain. It was as if the Almighty could have breathed life as easily into silicon as into carbon. Design and beauty teased each other. Inside this intimacy was the total control of all northern European information flows. Information is power. From a distance the edifice looked rather like a gigantic earth-bound jellyfish. Its huge dome dominated the Fenland skyline. Trinity College, Cambridge had founded a science park in the 1970s and through such firms as Acorn and ARM the 'Silicon Fens' had been born. With so much local expertise it was an ideal place to build Inflow.

The structure was surrounded by a moat and rose 80 stories high. The vast roof created its own micro-climate which kept icy winds or harsh sun at bay. Fronds hung down from its edge acting like a curtain which came alive in the wind. These fronds were also sophisticated defence against rogue aircraft flying into the central column as they had done into the Twin Towers in New York at the turn of the century. The dome's surface concealed a myriad of aerials pointing to information sources. It glowed in colours to match and contrast with weather conditions; as the sun set over Ely Cathedral so Inflow picked up golds and pinks but added green and blue tints.

The locals called it the Fish. It had an underground security complex which few understood. Inflow members hardly noticed that their subconscious behaviour was observed. Privacy was a thing of the past. Each person's habits were known and constantly monitored. If anyone was embarrassed or uneasy security knew.

George worked for security which was why he was monitoring Io. She dried herself after her swim; questioning unsettled her. 'What am I doing with my life at the Fish? Why all this information? What are we doing with all this stuff anyway? Does it have any value or is it just making the world less real?' Io put another dried piece of dung on one of the fires encircling the pool. She sat on a rock watching and listening to the night. A gentle breeze wafted her hair. The aroma from the fires was pleasing, rather like a joss-stick but without the sweetness, and kept mosquitoes away. She had learnt about dung fires on her first visit to the tropics.

She kept quite still, thinking. The moon smiled down. The night sounds rose in volume as she let her mind run free. For some time this gentle girl had collected big questions which simmered in a pot at the back of her mind. Now was the moment she had prepared. George thought she must be into meditation. He studied her face through night sights. It was

3

unbearably hot in his protective suit, so quietly he removed headgear and gloves. The mosquitoes bit his face and hands. He hated insects.

Arthor had married Clairu at thirty. They were delighted when a year later their firstborn arrived. She had been delivered in the old-fashioned natural way. The birth had been painful but straightforward. The little babe's head was squashed out of shape but after a day or so recovered and seemed almost perfectly round. They had tried out various names but somehow these didn't suit their little daughter. Neither parent liked the idea of modifying name endings as in Arthor for Arthur or Clairu for Claire, neither did they want a common Christian name for her. In the end Io suited her round head and soft complexion. It also followed a convention of naming offspring after celestial bodies.

Proud parents worshipped their little daughter. Io grew strong and well. They longed for a companion sibling yet were unable to bring to birth another child. How could it be that their only child was so healthy and had been so easily conceived? Clairu had several miscarriages trying for another yet the option of buying a baby never crossed their minds. What Nature had decided was to be honoured, even though it cost dear in heartache. They relished nurturing Io in the Dorset countryside; she developed a love for the sea, both walking its cliffs and swimming in it. Respect for the natural became essential in her heart and mind. As she grew she was invited to allow 'question' and 'acceptance' to be equal partners in her life.

In the tropical moonlight she accepted that there was no longer such a thing as privacy. Had civilization come full circle? In warm climates clothes were unnecessary yet there was no embarrassment. Now that sophisticated surveillance techniques and digitized recognition software had taken away privacy, need there be any embarrassment? Her questions could have taken her to a therapist but Io inherently mistrusted professional advisers unless they were catalysts who inspired rather than shrinks who interrogated. Instead her questions took her to the tropics, to lands at ease with nature and unspoiled by so-called civilization. She had to get away from tourists, business, and busyness.

Her paternal great grandmother, Louise Smith had grown up in the tropics. Greatma had often spoken of the wild expanse of space getting into her blood. Io Smith inherited genetically and through nurture from Louise. That inheritance served her well. The first time she had been to the tropics was via a mission exchange. She was only fourteen but the friendships made were to stand the test of time. Io had become part of this wider 'family' and yearned for the spaces that could bring balm to her soul. Somehow the busyness at the Fish seemed like blowing in the wind. The real world was under this moonlight. Io was at peace; she stretched herself, climbed down from the rock to her tent and was soon fast asleep. George was now even more fascinated by her. He began to scratch the mosquito bites.

02 Thames' insight

The train pulled up gently and silently at London Liverpool Street. When the station had first been built dirty, noisy, living steam engines had sweated their way to the buffers. Now, almost ghostly carriages glided on plastic wheels to a standstill. No noise, no pollution, and little excitement. Gustav shepherded his adolescent flock to the bike racks. All except one freed a machine for the journey through the bronchs to the Tate Encounter. Ashley's pic didn't seem to work so Gustav released the bike himself hoping he would remember to transfer the charges to Ashley's account later.

Why was it always Ashley? There was something about the expression in his eyes that puzzled Gustav. Was he stupid or crafty? He was certainly intelligent. Gustav determined to realize rather than frustrate this intelligence. He made a cryptic note on his buddy which he had recently upgraded and fitted into his left shoe. He kept his sphinx in his right shoe and although his shoes communicated with each other Gustav liked some sense of control over his personal data and diary. He was suspicious of the combined sabs now available where sphinx and buddy were in one unit.

Gustav began to make his charges look at their environment. "Can you tell me when the bronchs were built and why? Do you think they have been a success, and what spin-offs have there been?"

Ashley was the first with sphinx and discovered that *in the 2020s pollution in large cities became so severe that a Royal Commission was called to make radical suggestions. The bronchs was one result. The bargain struck between city authorities and commuters was simple. If they could get to and from work at no cost to the environment then the city would provide them with clean air passages for travel. These air passages were called the bronchs after the passages to the human lungs. They were like motorways that had been designed for cyclists rather than cars. Cross winds, traffic interruptions, and rain were eliminated. The bronchs were the lungs of the city.*

They raced to the Tate, put their bikes in racks and savoured the artistic delights. The hologram dances were amazing. Two hours later they cycled down the Thames in a section of the bronchs half-covered by the incoming tide. It was fantastic passing under Tower Bridge towards Greenwich and the Time Track; the view just above the water was quite amazing.

Before the freshers entered the complex Gustav briefed them. "This place is based on an archaic and lazy design; however it still tells a good story. You can be taken around the time zones by museum transport but if you really want to think then walk and talk. I want you to answer this basic question. Why did China trigger the production of riders? And I don't want a sphinx type answer. The last time I asked a question about spin-offs from the creation of the bronch system you just gave me reasons for its genesis. You told me nothing about the morale of the city with people being fitter, liberated rather than frustrated in traffic jams. It has been a major force in the regeneration of city community. I expect better of you, so get behind the data to the wisdom it teaches! See you back here in two hours".

They disappeared relishing active learning rather than passive digestion of boring information. Peace at last, and time to think. Gustav had been to this place many times. The conveyor transport intensely annoyed his sense of learning. Despite regular correspondence with the authorities it remained in place. Their argument centred on equality of access for the disabled but Gustav wondered whether it was more about maximising throughput.

In one of his more creative moods he had sent messages by fountain pen on paper, and then by every other means invented since. Writing on paper was immensely satisfying although so slow. He still used it as an exercise for his students. Some had never seen ink before! Funnily enough it was his hand-written epistle that had produced the most response. It was one of two such messages received that year and was now framed as part of a display. The other correspondence was lost in statistical analysis showing that the majority of visitors preferred to be lazy.

William and Ashley paired off as usual. *China launched more satellites in the second decade of the twenty first century than either Europe (including Russia) or the US.* "Let's start at the turn of the century, Wills", suggested Ashley. The chase towards wisdom had begun.

Later they met in the sun beside the river. Gustav told them to pick up bikes for the bronchs down to the Thames Barrier. He had booked a floating conference room. Somehow to glide just above Old Father Thames created a sense of perspective. The river had seen so many changes but was largely unchanged itself. River traffic had reduced. The water of the Thames made air-conditioning efficient in summer and (via heat exchangers) was a source of heat in winter. Fresh air companies had sprung up along the bronchs pumping high quality air into the network, and also supplying local communities. Since the Hanoi Summit it was Earth policy that all such companies use sustainable energy sources.

Gustav called them a pod, not after peas all neatly arranged but after dolphins continuously leaping and taking turns to lead. He had no fixed number or type because he recognised that each intake of freshers was different. In this pod one girl, Pamela Smith, was joined by four boys. The mix worked well; they brought the best out in her: feminine intuition and persistence; and she encouraged them to be more thoughtful, to enjoy banter but also work as a focused team.

Alfred Cookson was the oldest at eighteen; he was one of those quiet people always present yet easily overlooked. He had spent most of his life in rural Suffolk and knew the Fens like the back of his hand. These country roots were proving invaluable to the pod. His colleagues had learnt to include quiet Cookson in their thinking.

They shared their findings with Gustav. China had scores to settle. The country had a vast population and ancient wisdom; yet the cocky so-called Western civilization treated them as somehow backward. Human rights was always the issue, but what record did the Western world portray? Beneath the veneer of decency was appalling poverty. The extremes between rich and poor were scandalous. There were no slaves in chains but there were many in economic bonds. How dare the West lecture China? And yet she did not wish to wage war, not conventional war. She would rule the ether by saturating geostationary orbits with her satellites. The West was suspicious and in turn launched supervisory satellites armed with sophisticated detection equipment and powerful lasers. Signals were monitored; if necessary these battleship satellites could fry any competition out of orbit.

Brussels made the first move in what would have been described in the nineteenth century as 'gunboat diplomacy'. China was ordered to share orbits or face the consequences. The Circinus launchers put up enough gunboat satellites to sort out China's entire fleet. It was of course the immature impetuous Americans who made the first mistake. During the Beijing Festival of China transmissions suddenly ceased. The cluster of Chinese satellites overhead were eliminated, all twelve of them. The fireworks display could be seen by the naked eye. Shrapnel was blasted in all directions. This volume of debris, even in the wide expanse of space, was to prove catastrophic.

This was the moment Gustav Kimmler relished. Soon the freshers would learn his style. It was immensely rewarding to watch wisdom blossom from data. It reminded him of the opening lines from Genesis where the Spirit of God turned the chaos into the beauty of Eden. The Spirit was wisdom. "I'll give a fountain pen and paper to the student who, in the judgement of all of us, produces the greatest wisdom - quality, not just quantity". His eyebrows played across the dark complexion of his boyish face. At only 27 years of age he was commanding considerable respect for his innovative methods.

"I think the satellites had a kind of remote war and destroyed each other", offered Zoid. "I bet it was a software fault that started it; always is". He couldn't help sounding superior; it was all that well-breeding. In fact Zoid Shevardnadze was a likeable lad with an appetite for learning. He didn't tolerate fools gladly. He came in for plenty of banter but stood up to it well. Only occasionally had Zoid been bullied and each time it had taught him to grow up. He wasn't frightened of a bit of rough and tumble. His first black eye had earned him respect. The son of new Russian money he'd been sent to the Waterbeach Metaguild largely on Gustav's reputation.

"Why start a satellite war if China's communications had already been downgraded?", asked Ashley. "What would be the point?"

"I wonder if sphinx can come up with anything". William asked a few questions and eventually found out that *at the turn of the century the power of the Western Allies was mocked by Saddam Hussein who had ruled Iraq with an iron fist. He particularly enjoyed tempting America to overreact. Every means to annoy was deployed by Saddam; he almost became respectable, even though he had been so brutal.*

"I reckon the Americans decided to finish off China's satellites completely to be sure she was unable to embarrass them as Iraq had done before. I still can't work out why everyone else's went down too. China didn't have attack weapons in space", puzzled Pamela.

She said little yet listened much. Her clear blue eyes looked at Gustav. Here was the fair, wise, confident goddaughter of Io Smith; it was a common surname but this particular branch showed uncommon prowess.

Gustav intervened, "You are working well but need to think laterally. I want to introduce you to Susan who has 102 years of wisdom". The freshers expected some new communications interface, but to their surprise an old woman's hologram was projected into the learning suite. "Susan and I have worked together for the last few years. She has remarkable insight, and I was ..."

The hologram laughed and Susan (who was walking around her lovely cottage garden in the Yorkshire Dales) said how much Gustav's invitation meant to her. The young girl inside her old frame still danced. Gustav continued, "I was delighted when Susan took up my invitation to act as my mentor, my elder. I once had a conversation with an African whose people had been caught up in a long and bitter civil war; their poverty was obscene. I asked him what the greatest difference was between our countries. I expected him to focus on wealth or peace. Adok replied that he was appalled by how we wasted the wisdom of our elders. As a result I approached Susan. Her wisdom may be a prize greater than wealth or peace".

Unexpectedly a hush fell on the freshers; they forgot their enthusiasm for a moment. They found Susan's hologram captivating. Here was a spirit that their young hearts sought. Here was living tradition. It was a revelation. The few seconds were a breach into eternity. Gustav sighed beyond himself, a primitive, secure sigh that was profoundly comforting. He was watching a divine movement.

Zoid's family was at home in the grandeur of events. The scale of his stately home gave him an almost genetic sense of confidence. Such was the true definition of an aristocrat. "Can you give us a clue Ma'am? We don't seem to be able to see what is in front of us".

"Let him who has eyes to see, see", began Susan. "When Marie Curie discovered radium she realized that she had found a substance which appeared to give out energy without itself being changed. She had eyes to see what appeared to be impossible. We now know that an irradiating substance does change by releasing some of its extraordinary nuclear energy. How do we harness that energy? That's your clue. I'm off to do some gardening, but call again if you want help. Meanwhile I'll carry on listening to your conversation. I hope Gustav had the courtesy to tell you that I was listening".

Gustav was embarrassed a moment and flushed slightly. He apologized to Susan who although saying nothing somehow acknowledged him by carrying on gardening.

"I thought she was going to give us the answer, not ask yet another question", complained Ashley. "Why did you call her Ma'am, Zoid. You're just a creep". His green eyes bore down on Zoid.

"Shut up, Ash. I like to find answers for myself", asserted Zoid firmly in his pristine English. "What was it she asked?"

Susan's intervention brought them insight. Nuclear energy was harnessed by setting up a chain reaction, and *the debris from China's destroyed satellites had set up a chain reaction destroying other satellites. The earth had been plunged into the equivalent of a communications ice-age. Geo-positioning systems no longer functioned; without satnavs people were lost because few could map-read. Only land based systems worked but they were so overloaded and slow that information was trimmed to the essentials of banking, security, and shopping. The earth community had shot itself it the foot in a big way. The rider network had been created to replace satellites and was based upon experiments carried out by Google over New Zealand in 2013.*

"What is the wisdom in all this?" persisted Gustav. This time blue eyes spoke, "I reckon wisdom was rediscovered when mass communication was lost". Susan's hologram suddenly reappeared; "That's very profound, Pamela. I reckon you're a candidate for the pen and ink".

"A breakthrough. Insight. Great; it's been a good morning's work. Thanks. Time to relax. See you back here in one point seven hours, or if you like you can join Susan and me for lunch". Gustav's charges melted away. Here was a moment for him to learn again from a very wise woman.

03 Bronchs meeting

'The snake is not evil, it is crafty,' thought George. Being in security suited him down to the ground. His feline instinct to stalk was immensely rewarded, yet there was a cost. Security personnel were not supposed to get involved with Inflow members. The snake logo and motto 'Be crafty not evil' were reminders to value neutrality. Nevertheless what harm would there be in closer observation of Io?

He would invite her out. It would have to be on some pretext because no doubt George was being observed too. But where and how? George was by nature passive; others were his stimuli. Oh yes, he appeared active and his stealth prowess had been noted by his seniors. Yet at moments like this he found it difficult to marshal an argument and even more difficult to make a decision. It bugged him.

Io had formidable power over George. She presented the challenge; she puzzled him; how could she be so innocent and yet not naïve? Whiter than snow, or a mirage of clear water in his parched desert? They were poles apart in temperament; what bound them was restlessness. Io was disturbed by her role at Inflow, and George was disturbed by Io.

Io had had enough after a busy day's work and took a lift down to the bronchs station at the base of the Fish. She changed into her cycling gear and was soon in the warm exit branch travelling under the moat to emerge into the fading autumn light. She banked left

15

along the Cut-off Channel and underneath the railway. As she gained speed her body warmed up so that it felt comfortable reaching the cooler air of the mainline bronch at Hiss Farm, and then running south west parallel to the trains. It wasn't too busy; she switched on her lights and was soon lost in thought, unwinding at her normal cruising speed of 22mph.

George had to peddle hard to catch up with Io; her silhouette was now in sight as the bronch crossed the Lark river. He wouldn't have much time because in a few minutes the branch to Ely would take her away from him. Io first noticed George as a distracting combination of panting and thudding. Sweat was pouring off his face.

"What's the rush? Just enjoy the ride". He struggled to respond. She slowed a little to cool down ready for Ely.

They cycled in silence but the thudding annoyed her. "Your tyre has a bald patch".

He laughed. "What's so funny?" He took a big breath, "Your blond hair is a trailing hazard". She reached up and felt around the back of her helmet but no golden locks had escaped. He laughed again.

"Touché. By the way, I'm Io; we haven't met before have we?"

"No", he lied. He had met her in his dreams; the tropical moonlight haunted him. Somehow George felt embarrassed in pretending ignorance. "I'm George. Are you from these parts?", he asked tamely.

"Not originally. Inflow invited me to join them after discovering some of my beaches. For some reason they displayed 'design integrity' because the scenes were so natural yet every part led to more information. Anyway I was invited over for an interview and some teamwork tests, and then given a starting share at the Fish. What do you do?"

"I'm in liability management; we analyse systems to find any weak links and then ..." Io was irritated and suspicious, "Go on with you! How long have you worked for security?" George went through the routine he had learnt in training. He deliberately misheard 'in securities' rather than 'for security'.

"Oh no, not securities, although that's part of it. I'm in risk management". Io could see through the rhetoric but thought it wise not to push her luck. "Oh, I see".

It had rained for weeks so the Great Ouse river was full; a few fields were flooded. The bronch dipped from the railway line down to the north bank of the swollen river. The Ely junction appeared and Io moved into the slip lane. "See you again sometime, George".

He cycled on angry that a conversation that had begun so promisingly and naturally had ended in silence. But Io's parting shot was generous and gave him hope. He increased his pace and arrived at his Cambridge home dripping with sweat, exhausted, and vowing next time to take the train between home and Ely. He would see her again, and on brand new tyres.

"Hey, Blondie, how come you're so fit?" Io was cycling in her bright purple and green striped suit and George had let her begin to overtake him. Inflow tracking had told him via his buddy when she would be on the Ely branch before joining the Cam bronch towards Lakenheath and the Fish. Her image on his visor's map allowed him to cycle slightly ahead of her, but slow enough to be caught. It was a week after their first meeting. She responded well to his teasing greeting; in fact the banter gave her freedom to skirt around him, to find out what made him tick. The river was still full as they cycled over it and up the gradual incline to run beside the railway line.

"If you call me Blondie, I shall call you Georgie Porgie. How come you're not panting like last time?". He was pleased she noticed and replied in an off-hand manner. "Oh, that's because I caught the train from home to Ely, otherwise 30 miles is a bit far even inside a bronch".

He amused her. They cycled together at a slightly slower pace - more breath for conversation. "What have you been up to this past week, apart from getting new tyres?"

George had anticipated the question. How could he admit to watching her, to collecting as much security information as possible from confidential backups? He had toyed with an alibi but knew she could see through him. The pause was just about to be broken by Io, who wondered if he had heard her properly, when he asked, "When we last met, why did you think I worked for security?"

Although coming straight to the point Io was gracious in her manner. "Well, you try too hard. What I mean is that you can tell by your manner, by your bearing. Then when you pretend otherwise it makes it even more obvious". She did not want to run George down; after all he might be able to help her sort out some of her puzzles. The trouble with working at Inflow was that you were always on the inside. One of her reasons for travelling by bronch rather than train was to have time to think. The trains, although much faster, were almost an extension of the Fish. George might be a useful inside outsider!

The bronchs had the great advantage of being clear all around so the autumn colours could be savoured. After the Ely bend the section running parallel to the railway was straight for miles until Lakenheath and the Fish. Wheels spun; legs and arms pulled and pushed rhythmically. The breeze intermingled with conversation; hearts pumped oxygen riches to muscle and mind. Quick wits, humour, and energy whirled around exploring new vistas of spirit, of life, of adventure. Their souls made the banks of a stream which flowed not with water but with words, pictures, ideas, and mystery. There was some chemistry between them.

The communications jellyfish iridescent on Fenland horizon was now rearing above, dominating the sky. The human soul was reduced to bee-like proportions in this hive driven by a hungry world desperate for the honey of information; for what? ... for why? She found herself squeezed by the atmosphere; he felt at home. They had agreed to meet again.

Io slowed her pace at Hiss Farm as they entered the cool inward bronch running beneath the security moat into the heart of the Fish; George kept up his speed to get there first, and took a shower. She appreciated the simple but effective cooling design for cyclists as she parked her bike, detached her bag, hooked her helmet, and the purple and green outfit over the handlebars; she pushed a button and all was whisked away into a secure rack. A lift took her to the 59th floor; Io yawned to balance the air pressure in her ears and stepped out into her workspace for another pointless day.

04 Snug hiss

Silvanus was the result of a wild romance between a buxom tea-lady and a professor of psychology. Sounds crazy but then many things appeared crazy to Cynthia. That wasn't her real name but it suited her because she felt synthetic. She looked good although little of the original remained; the wonders of modern science! Let's fill out some detail here. Tea-ladies had been phased out in the 1970s only to be replaced by machines and plastic cups. Old folk sang out how much they missed the personal touch and the anticipation of an approaching trolley.

Then along came some bright spark who rediscovered the tea-lady. Tea-gentlemen didn't catch on in spite of mandatory gender-bias tests pedantically executed. In the past an era of 'political correctness' had assumed male and female to be so boringly similar that you almost wondered why the Almighty had invented them in the first place.

And so we come to the professor. Tea could be produced chemically by mechanical means without emotion. Tea-ladies combined the mechanics with sociological counselling skills (mothering?), firm discipline validated by respect gained rather than imposed through management structure, and last but by no means least a folk link with the past. Here was tannin in the form of real ale. Tea from the cask; none of your plastic wrapped lager rubbish on this trolley. Irresistible to Professor Montague Woodlander.

And Silvanus, the seed of this delightfully

disastrous parentage, was a crafty bastard absorbed by his thirst for power.

The snug was comfortably furnished in traditional style with two leather sofas and some chairs arranged around a tatty oak table. Silvanus had a diverse membership to his Cell. They would gather at a hostelry named 'Five Miles From Anywhere' which was very popular to those who could find it. Regulars travelled out from Ely; there were always tourists attracted to the romantic spot where the three Lodes of Wicker, Burwell and Reach empty into the river Cam. 'Jack Frost' had painted the fens with ice and crystal; the lodes were frozen over. The pub included a bar for locals who rarely ventured from the Fens; they were fond of their brass sign 'Grumpies' screwed to the rough oak beam overhead.

The Cell had gathered at Silvanus' request (a command really) to have a jar at 'The Five'. The room was relaxing but strangely quiet; the low reflective ceiling allowed conversation at minimum volume. The door was behind one of the bookcases which swung open when activated by Silvanus. No one could quite remember how they had gained entry.

Silvanus had designed his snug to be at the centre of a block of debugged rooms, rather like Rubik's Cube invented in the 1970s; nobody could ever see the centre because it was always screened by outside cubes. Trial release of sensitive but useless information had not registered on the swell. Silvanus felt safe in his snug. He controlled access. In here you would never know the depths of winter outside.

He addressed his Cell in riddles, "I'm not playing about here - and neither are you. Minds can wander, secrets spill but so does blood. You know, but never know. I always know".

"Honey", interrupted his shapely girlfriend Jeanette, "can you explain what the hell you mean?" She wasn't the sharpest tool in the box, so Silvanus used her question as a convenient opportunity to draw breath before continuing.

"Hardware can be seen by ultrasound or whatever but software is more subtle. You know that Christmas party we had last week at Tuddenham Mill. OK, you were too stoned or pissed to remember; that's the point, you can't remember".

"Good party Boss, but if we can't remember nout why bring it up now?" queried Victor as he scratched his beard and blinked rapidly through a rather heavy set of glasses. He enjoyed traditional ales.

"You brought enough up at the time, Victor", said Charles, a contented bachelor with a wild mop of fair hair.

"The elephants don't wish to know", quipped Victor, but Silvanus cut him off, "And neither do I".

He treated the chatter as space for thought rather than conversation. But Silvanus had a canny knack of knowing when an important point was raised; it wasn't now though. His was a style of conversation that gave the impression of lighthearted intercourse, but he was quite ruthless in driving to his destiny.

"You can't remember that I brought you by taxi one at a time to this snug. It wasn't just the drink; the anaesthetic draught helped knock out your minds and in particular the feeling in your wrists". A Freudian reaction from Silvanus' Cell made them rub their wrists as a chill ran down their spines. A clammy fear gripped them as they gripped their wrists. This kind of poetry in motion warmed Silvanus to his theme. How quickly the mood could change. They say tears and laughter are close; mirth and mistrust hand in hand.

"Your pics have been replaced. I have the originals here". Silvanus held up a small flask. "They were used to programme the replacements in your wrists, but I've added software. I've added", Silvanus repeated himself for affect and dropped his voice, "I've added a Silvanus special. Nothing can detect it, but it lets me know what you're up to".

"Bullshit, Silvanus", laughed Victor hoping to push the conversation towards banter. "You expect us to believe that".

"Yes, Victor old chap. You can show the others but one of them will have to show you".

"Go on then ...", but Victor stopped suddenly. The chill down his spine was real this time. It was as if his head floated above a body which he knew supported it but of which he could feel nothing. He kept breathing but seemed to freeze in time as he slumped back into the sofa. The others didn't notice at first for he seemed to be day dreaming. Conversation continued for a moment until everyone looked at Victor.

"I forgot to tell you about your neck implants", Silvanus lied. "Your modified pics remotely control a kind of artificial hormone system in your blood stream. The implants freeze your spinal chord whenever I decide. Handy because I can immobilise you but your faculties

24

remain active. You're the best bugs in the business".

"You bastard, Silvanus. You mean to say that you have fixed all of us, even me, your own father?" Montague's anger was tempered by fear; there was a wanton ruthlessness about Silvanus which had an appetite of its own. What kind of son had he and Cynthia produced?

"Yes. Yes, I have. And no one will ever know because my stealth software can't be detected. It's stealth we are about. By the way, any interference with your neck implants will release sufficient toxin to paralyse you for life". It wasn't true but he knew they wouldn't take the risk; the possibility was deterrent enough.

They hated Silvanus, yet they loved his power because it gave them purpose, it gave them life.

"Riders are like red blood cells in this tinpot planet's comms network. They transport the oxygen of information around as they drift on their stratospheric currents. White cells are the military, always on the lookout for subterfuge. We, to be more accurate you, are going to infiltrate the riders. You're about stealth. How are you going to do it?"

Silvanus switched Victor back on but nobody could quite see how he did it. "Victor, now your rigor mortis is over, what do you think?" Victor rubbed his neck. "Can I stand and walk about; I feel all stiff?"

"Yes brains! And loosen up your mind at the same time. And you Spaniel; get your nose on that scent boy". Charles Jarman had been nicknamed Spaniel by Silvanus when he learnt of his old-fashioned monarchist views. "Come on King Charles, the Spaniel", he would tease. It was a bit twee, and at first it rankled with him but now he had been effectively domesticated by the Silvanus' aura. For relaxation Charles took part in battle re-enactments and if possible would always choose a royalist role.

His strategic insight was uncanny in its power and simplicity. Many became absorbed by detail, not so with Charles who paused, as was his wont, before beginning, "Last century, in the 1980s, at the height of the Cold War, a young man took off in a small domestic aeroplane and flew through all the fancy radar detection equipment to land safely in Moscow's Red Square. Many a theft has been carried out in broad daylight by crooks posing as normal removal men".

A grin crept across Silvanus' flat ugly face. The tree-man was amused. Here was the key he had been looking for. It all fitted so well. "Go on, Spaniel, I like it. Might re-christen you St Peter, the saint with all the keys". He laughed and the Cell relaxed a little. They broke for coffee.

05 Courting

Cooped up in an airless cell George and Io battled a game of brawn and brain. The ball flicked over wooden floor, smashed from wall to wall beneath top court lines until managing to hide from their racquets in a corner. Points were registered and the score relayed by audio as the screen updated. It was a good match. Io insisted that she be given no handicap. The squash ball was hollow; no programme. George won easily. He had the better technique. She felt his stalking skills as those sharp eyes noted her every move. Surprise seemed impossible. How could she improve? He made her competitive.

After a shower, cool in the bar, she quizzed him. How did he know her game so easily. He kept mum. She determined to find out. George diverted the subject. "Tell me about the tropics". How did he know? She racked her brain to try and remember if she had ever talked about the place where her spirit was free. It seemed a million miles away from Cambridge in the depth of winter. She became angry and confused but tried to appear at ease because she wanted to both protect her space from his gaze, and to find out what he was doing there. Now she knew it had been a man watching her bathe in the tropical moonlight.

"I'm not really in the mood now, George". He had only brought the subject up as a diversion, but he had made a big mistake. She now knew he was from security and had been researching her. All their growing friendship might be just duty for him, using her to extract more data. He felt dirtied by his job. Security's motto 'Be crafty not evil' flashed across his mind. He wondered if it was possible. He loved Io for her integrity, for her beauty, for her fun, for who she was. He didn't want to mess it all up. They agreed to a match the following week and to meeting on the bronch the day before.

That night Io slept fitfully. The squash had tired her physically but Georgie Porgie had put her mind in a whirl. She had to admit that she had grown rather fond of him, yet there was something in his manner that annoyed her. It was as if he was chasing her by letting her take initiatives and reacting to them. Fair enough, the gentlemen often chased the ladies who would run just fast enough to be caught. She knew that game, but just at the moment she was in no mood to be caught. She needed to win.

George too found that sleep did not come easily. Io was not a woman who could take the leading role in his romantic dreams. There was more to her than tickling his fancy. Somehow he felt summoned before her to give account. She was his queen.

In the morning before peddling off to work Io noted down a few ideas for the next game of squash. On the swell she found a hologram tutor for her return home. And George, so as not to appear too suspicious, took the train to Lakenheath. He determined to come clean next time he met the comely Blondie.

The Panton Arms served free range veal thinly sliced in a beautiful port sauce. The vegetables were delicious: parsnip lightly fried in butter, mange-tout peas, baked sprouts and sweet potatoes. Small Yorkshire puddings, crisp on the outside but gloriously soggy on the inside adorned the edge of their plates. The atmosphere was between town and gown. An open fire burned brightly. Io and George were in the mood for a good meal and also eager for conversation. It seemed ages since they had really talked. Both wanted to move on from their combative squash court encounters.

"This is lovely George. Thanks. It's been a busy week and I need to relax". Typically English, George replied, "Oh don't mention it". He was thrilled she had. What a beautiful woman; what a beautiful person. He was quite in awe.

"Tell me about your family, George", came a gentle instruction from Io. He waited for a moment, slightly fazed. His family were as English as English could be. The Freemans went back a long way. Education was a strand that held them together. His parents met at Oxford where they were both reading law. Father read law and music, mother read law with French. George had an autistic brother Basil, who although six years his senior appeared to have an emotional age of eleven. He lived unhappily in a hostel; this was a deep disappointment to the family because they had tried to keep Basil at home but it nearly broke them. The hostel cared for him satisfactorily yet his unhappiness hung over the Freemans. As George spoke Io was moved by his anguish and volunteered a trite encouragement.

"You've never really known a seriously autistic person have you", commented George quietly. "Basil's personality is radically different from ours. To put it simply, he is both child and adult; if you try to bring him together it is like tearing him apart. On the other hand what is normal for him is abnormal and uncomfortable for us. He tears us apart because we don't have his ..." George couldn't find the right word; he wanted to be true to Basil. "We don't have his gift".

There was a wholesome pause. Io had the sense to keep quiet. George slowly drank half a glass of rosé and when he put the glass down she lent forward and laid her hand on his; "Thank you".

It was true companionship. George did not feel patronised; he was not sure she understood about Basil but she understood him. He turned his hand to hold hers and caressed it gently with his thumb. "Perhaps you will meet him one day".

"I'd like that". They ordered sweet, and Io teased that plum pudding wasn't on the menu.

"What about your family?" Io took a deep silent breath and leant back. She told him she was the only child of Arthor and Claru whom she dearly loved and respected. They had their funny ways but were wise and young at heart. She regularly visited them in Dorset, and they stayed for long weekends with her in Ely. Her goddaughter Pamela was only sixteen but as bright as a button, and she had just joined the Waterbeach Metaguild under the amazing Gustav Kimmler. It was odd that Microsoft should have put up so much money for an institution centred on wisdom and excellence. Their track record in the early years of computing had been for mass-marketed second rate technology. Anyway that was another story.

One of the greatest influences on Io was Greatma. She was a free spirit. Born Louise Freak she had married Robert to become a Smith. Now aged ninety five she was physically fit, taking into account half a dozen new joints. The couple lived in a corner flat overlooking Brighton Pier, and were still quite independent knowing that their son and daughter-in-law lived a short distance away nearer the railway station.

"By the way George, how did you know I had been to the tropics?" The question came out of the blue yet it was a relief to George. He had determined to come clean with Io. He marvelled at her wide ranging temper. One minute relishing family values and the next interrogating the accused. She was dangerous, a true Smithy. One minute warming iron, the next beating it out on a cold hard anvil.

"This is dangerous for me. You know that I work for Inflow security. They will be watching me to make sure we do not compromise each other". He shuffled awkwardly in his chair. "I wouldn't compromise you, Porgie", quipped Io.

"Listen, you don't understand ..." He sighed. "I have always played by their rules until now. I am already compromised just by seeing you, unless I can justify it on security grounds". George went on to tell Io that her restlessness had been detected and that he had been instructed to watch her, the comely maiden, swimming in the tropical moonlight months before.

She surprised him by revealing that she somehow knew that she was being watched then, and that it was a relief to know who had been her mystery observer. She went on to explain how he might help her understand why she was restless. They talked of travelling back from Africa, Southern Sudan to be precise; she had flown to Marseilles and then caught Eurostar to St Pancras. He had been flown directly to Inflow's Lakenheath runway.

George found passion in his voice; he was almost shaking with emotion. "The trouble is Io, I have grown very fond of you. Let me see your blue eyes … I am drawn by your lovely eyes, by you. I am afraid that I will come to love you".

Io blushed but without awkwardness. "George, I'm fond of you but I don't want to rush things. Who knows, love may blossom but let's give each other space. Sorry, I must sound like Greatma Smith. I hadn't realized about the cost for you in all this. It may be good for us though".

It was a good meal: food, conversation, honesty. Outside the cold air played briefly with each breath as it caught the starlight. They planned to meet more but were going to have to be careful where. The bronchs were safe. Thank God for the bronchs.

06 Pondering

Ashley Woodlander and William Inchbald were thick besides being bright. They had a certain chemistry about them. Each was a catalyst to the other. Ashley's quest for advantage gave him a restlessness which somehow suited his ginger features. Most found him intense and claustrophobic; however William was so used to it that he virtually ignored the traits. They had had a few blazing rows which resulted in an understanding which gave space for each other's opinion.

"Did you watch that game last night, Wills? That try by Firano was fantastic. He programmed the ball just right". His freckled face screwed up slightly, adding unnecessary tension to an ordinary question.

"No, I was out with Mum and Dad. They had been working together on a dialect recognition programme and hadn't been out of the house for days. They were getting ratty so I told them they needed a break. Couldn't believe it when they took notice of me".

"Pity. You missed a cool game. What did you do with the oldies anyway, Wills?" They walked along the Cam river as they talked; William taking short frequent steps.

"We went down to the new Sports Entirety gym; it's impressive. You really do feel able to compete on equal terms without the virtual being too strong. You actually come off the court sweating".

"Sounds cool. How do you vary the virtual then?" William explained how you warmed up on a trial setting and then had the first game. Depending on the result you arrived at a handicap setting. Play began in earnest with all the players reducing virtual to a minimum. The best players had hardly any virtual at all.

Ashley's father, Silvanus Woodlander, had seeded a child by Holly when she was only seventeen. He had been impatient with having a family at first, but seemed to settle and married Holly when their firstborn was two and was baptized, in fact it had been a joint occasion. Because they had been together for some time a grand white wedding seemed inappropriate, so a small village church sufficed and everyone walked there in wellington boots which were left in a random pile in the porch. It had all seemed so right to Silvanus at the time. How appropriate that a young girl called Holly should become a part of the Woodlander tribe. After all, his sister had been called Arborea.

When Ashley was only seven his parents split up and he came to know what heartache meant for the first time. It had been as if he had been cut in two emotionally while remaining physically intact. His little head could not, would not understand. He lived from Sunday to Wednesday in Lakenheath with his mother Holly, and the rest of the week in Eriswell with his so-called father Silvanus. The tear of his parents parting was bad enough; now it was reinforced by an arrangement permanently dividing him. He had had no say in all this because at seven he was deemed too young. It was young enough to be hurt but too young it seemed to be loved. As a result he buried himself in another world. 'Adventure' and 'discovery' became his parents. William became a kind of brother in Ashley's new 'family.'

When Ashley had cautiously dared to trust his new 'brother' the pair became almost inseparable. Sometimes others could not get a look in; they could only speak to them rather than to each individually. William Inchbald's parents had given wise counsel when he first met Ashley. They felt their parental love drawn through their precious and only son towards the heart-broken ginger lad.

Ashley had felt a sense of betrayal when his father's girlfriend Jeanette fell pregnant. She only lived a few streets away from his mother Holly. At full term Jeanette gave birth to healthy twins. Although Silvanus and Jeanette named them loosely in the Woodlander tradition it was clear early on that Silvanus did not want Fern and Ernest living with him at his Eriswell cottage. However he did regularly visit them and provided sufficient funds so that Jeanette only needed to work half-time in Inflow PR services while their twins attended pre-school; she looked after them the other half of the week.

"Can you be 100% healthy, Wills, or is it like infinity, impossible to reach?" Ashley initiated a completely new thread of conversation as the boys sat down with two freshly brewed mugs of red bush tea, a taste they had learnt from their inspirational Metaguild history tutor Gustav Kimmler.

"Well, what do you mean by health? Pete says health involves all that makes us human: body, mind, soul, and strength". He hadn't quite known how to respond so plucked an idea from a recent conversation he had had with Peter Roberts, the Metaguild chaplain.

"Getting all religious again! Why do you take so much notice of Pete anyway? Why don't you think for yourself, Wills old man?" There was a barb to his question but it was also genuine, longing for some solid rock in the shifting sands of his life.

"You're jealous! When you really want to know, I'll explain about models and faith, but right now you asked me about health. Ash, what do you want health, or faith, or both?" Previously William Inchbald would not have responded so strongly, but he had learnt that the passive conversation of his loving parents was not always the right mode for the freckled Ashley Woodlander.

"Sorry, no offence. I know it's real for you. OK, tell me about health". Before replying William smiled at Ashley and winked. They treasured their remarkable gift of robust thoughtful respectful exchange. "I will in a moment but I'm going to tell you why Chaplain Roberts helps me. He's integrated and has integrity! Besides his Metaguild role he is part of the Healthy Neighbourhood practice, and vicar to Waterbeach".

Ashley remained silent; part of what made their bond so strong was that the boys really argued and really listened. William went on, "It's a bit like computers with hardware, software, firmware, and all those other wares. One bit affects another. By the way I reckon some things just have to be received because you can only find them, not understand them!"

The trust and rapport between them was stunning. They had a respect for each other beyond their years. As they sparred they drew not blood but nuggets of wisdom.   Most wrote the pair off as living in another world, as nerds; but Gustav saw them as the first real potential for his research into wisdom.   His basic thesis was that she was available to all ages and in all situations. Mankind had lost the art of listening to her.

"As we progress, the boundary between natural biological life and artificial processes seems to be fading", argued William.   "Think of those replacement nerves your Gran had fitted last week. She is already showing sign of beginning to walk again. Is that health, Ash? The oldies keep asking when all the artificial is going to stop but they're first in the queue for replacements".

There was a long pause as the lads pondered a moment of Darwinian weight.   Could evolution of the human species include material that wasn't biological? *When mankind first went to the moon technology was so primitive that in order to reduce the weight of computers smaller logic circuits were designed. The first type used germanium but it was too temperature sensitive. Silicon logic circuits were first produced in the 1960s.*

"Think how much has happened since then, Ash. Microchips used to be enormous because of binary counting methods but now ..."

"What do you mean 'binary'?", puzzled Ashley. "It was a complete system of logic using 'on' or 'off'; it was so crude that logic operations took ages".

"Oh yes, I remember, that's partly why counting based on twelve was introduced. We should have been born with twelve fingers and toes. Ten can't be divided by three without getting recurring decimals".

"Point three three ... forever you mean".   There

was another short silence before William continued shouting in excitement. "That's it! I've got it! Hey, écoute mon ami!" They animatedly discussed how if biological selection improved species why shouldn't non-biological selection also work in the same way. Had mankind evolve beyond biology by thinking not in tens but in dozens? "We need to ask Gustav what he thinks". They went off to find him.

Two years before, Gustav had welcomed them as freshers to Waterbeach Metaguild. "If I can begin with our style; 'meta' as in 'metamorphosis' is the Greek for change; hence, metaguild is education in transition. Guilds are centres of craft, of wisdom. You come in here green having mastered 'the white heat of technology' but naïve in its use. Technology has tamed you; now you must become its master. By the way, sphinx will tell you who first used the 'white heat' image".

Alfred had anticipated the invitation and sphinx informed him through his contact lenses that *Prime Minister Harold Wilson used the phrase 'white heat of technology' as in this clip from one of his party political broadcasts in 1966 ...*

Gustav loved education. Information bored him as it did most others. Nerds were few nowadays; education had come of age in the techno era. Our little technological toys had in the past been tin gods inviting us to wallow in data, 'brilliant with information,' a phrase coined by Ray Bradbury in his prophetic novel 'Fahrenheit 451'. We had often wasted the wisdom of our elders or had rejected the past.

Education had been renewed and Gustav relished

his part in that renewal. "I see, when it comes to sphinx, you have the inside lane Alfred. Good, but you come to metaguild like fat caterpillars stuffed with facts gleaned from the cabbage-like sphinx plant. I want you to transform, to metamorphose into gossamer-light butterflies born on the winds of beauty, art, creation, and spirit".

That brief introduction had captivated William and Ashley. Gustav was more than a teacher; he was a companion on a journey discovering the intimacy of wisdom and her innate beauty. He understood their quest and he had a love of all disciplines not just one. He was the master physician and the others merely specialists. He could see the whole picture while they saw only through their particular specialism. If he had a weakness it was that he saw education as queen not knave.

Where would they find him this time of day? Gustav was not a creature of habit but neither was he an absentminded professor. Enquiry at reception yielded direction to the scented garden behind the cricket pavilion. Gustav had imported the idea from the Botanical Gardens at Cambridge. It appealed to his overall philosophy that boundaries are usually artificial. Wisdom could come to you through all the senses, including smell.

He was sitting, breathing deeply when Ashley and William arrived full of excitement. Gustav's passion was disciplined; although interruption was the last thing he wanted he knew these lads were on to something. How often people artificially created moments to talk? But conversation chooses its own moment usually at an inconvenient time and often late at night. This was such a moment.

Young lads are not partial to flower scent, yet Gustav invited them to sit down and breath deeply. "Take a moment to collect your thoughts so you can express them succinctly". They duly obeyed but wondered why he asked them to wait. Still, he usually had reasons.

"What's that smell?" asked the boys. "I'm glad you've noticed. This scented garden somehow puts my thoughts into perspective. Well, let's hear you".

They put their thesis to Gustav. Were silicon and carbon evolution systems the same? He paused for a moment and then began thinking aloud about deterrence. Ashley and William listened because they had learnt that he often approached an answer from an unexpected direction. It was this unpredictability that made Gustav such an inspiration.

He compared the complex and vastly expensive deterrence systems keeping the continental power blocks in check with the surveillance and locks for an ordinary house. The difference in scale made the comparison look ridiculous but in fact the principle of deterrence was exactly the same.

"I reckon that it's no different when it comes to evolution. If the processes that are behind the development of carbon based organisms are the same as those behind the silicon revolution then they are both evolutionary".

This was the cue they had been waiting for. Gustav had thrown a conclusion into the ring and they knew he now wanted their take on it. "But is it natural?" asked Ashley. "What I mean is who or what is in control?" He paused not quite understanding what he wanted to ask and yet at the same time knowing he was near the heart of the matter.

"Go on", encouraged Gustav, relishing the scent and the chase. "Well, if you buck Mother Nature she has a tendency to hit back. You know, all that stuff last century when the food chain was messed about because herbivores were given meat products and suddenly humans developed all kinds of odd diseases. Now with silicon there's no limit to its advance. Zoid has fancy implants in his eyes and ears so he can link to sphinx 24/7". Gustav thought for a while and then seemingly changed the direction of conversation to bees.

"A queen bee is natural, and yet how appalling that she should become an egg factory. If Mother Nature could do that then perhaps the excesses of biotechnology were more natural than they might appear. Now of course the trade-off in the evolution of the queen bee is that her every need is sated by attendant bees. I think this trade-off principle should be at the heart of any earth diplomacy leading to treaties covering gene modification or bionic implant".

No doubt the conversation would continue but for now Gustav needed space and invited the boys to leave him a while.

07 Brighton evening

The span of years helped but so did the span of generations. Io appreciated her roots and, perhaps because she was an only child, she regularly called on and relished the company of her elders. This was particularly so when she was out of sorts; their wisdom gave her fresh perspective, and their collective years of experience put her quarter century into context.

It was dark and cold: she zipped her leather jacket tight around her neck and walked past the museum and cathedral to the Ely station. So much cycling to the Fish and back through the bronch developed one set of muscles, walking emphasized a different combination and it was quite relaxing. There was a spring in her step.

The frost as the sun rose across Soham Lode was stunning. The train was soon past Waterbeach and pulled up at Cambridge where George joined; he climbed into a different coach and walked through the train until he found Io at a table seat pouring out two cups of tea from a large thermos.

In 35 minutes the train had reached London. Io had chosen Kings Cross station over Liverpool Street because the trip was faster and, so early on a Saturday, cheaper. They picked up bikes and cycled up the gentle incline from the platform into the bronch system. George had never been on the section to Victoria but Io knew it well and relished the banked corners as they swung past the British Museum, through Soho, around Buckingham Palace, and down onto the Brighton platform at Victoria station. Most of the bronch was at second storey height; Io loved the views and speed, while George concentrated to keep her in sight. It only took quarter of an hour.

Ten minutes later they were heading across the Thames towards Brighton. The train was comfortable and George felt peckish after the ride. Io had brought one banana which they shared as she warned him about Granny Smith's famous hospitality; they wouldn't starve.

The three great roof spans of the 1840 Brighton railway station welcomed them. George had never been there before and warmed to its style. Io suggested they walked down Queen's Road towards the sea, its fresh air a pleasant change from an air-conditioned railway coach.

After a short distance they crossed the road and entered into a building once operated by BBC Brighton, numbers 40-42 to be precise. They took a lift to the penthouse flat which overlooked the rooftops towards the sea. Io's paternal grandparents Siman and Janu Smith made them feel most welcomed; soon a large tray with coffee and cake was placed before them in the garden which was the pride and joy of their hosts.

Both in their mid-seventies they had plenty of creative energy. Siman explained that when they bought the flat it had potential for a garden but required careful construction so that no roots or leakage affected floors below. Janu said it was a combination of privacy and the central location near the station which drew them to their retirement home.

"And there's another even more important reason. Let's see if they are having coffee too. You'll need to come inside". She drew back the curtains from a window into her in-law's flat. Through it you could see an elderly couple sitting in separate wicker chairs looking out over Brighton Pier.

"Hello Greatma. I told you Io and her boyfriend George would be visiting us this weekend. Here they are!" Louise and Robert were in their late nineties with faces given great character by time's artistry. Their chairs swivelled round to face the window.

"Hello Io dear. You look so fit and healthy ... and this must be George. Very nice to see you. I hope you'll both call in while you're here. Would tomorrow morning after Church be any good?" Louise liked to have things organized.

"We'd love to Greatma", and turning towards Janu, Io checked, "If that's alright with you Gran?"

"Yes, of course it is. Do have a word with Robert". He was noticeably more frail than his wife and content to let her make arrangements. Yet when he spoke his eyes twinkled, as if the youngsters imparted some of their youthful energy to him.

"George, we mustn't let the women do all the talking. Do you mind me asking what you do for a living, or are you 'in between jobs' as they say?" George had dreaded the question but had an answer ready in his mind.

"I've been working with Inflow at Lakenheath for a number of years and commute in from Cambridge". He hoped that the last phrase would divert them from what he actually did, and the gamble paid off.

"You don't cycle all that away do you George?" asked Louise. "It must be all of 25 miles". Before replying George thought to himself that there were no flies on this set of Io's great grandparents.

"No, I usually get the train as far as Ely and then cycle into the Fish with Io. We can have a good chat on the way and keep trim at the same time".

"Well George", interjected Robert, "You'll need to do a few extra miles once Janu has finished with you. You'll be plum full of her tantalising cakes and soggy meringues".

George wondered for a moment if Io had passed on her nickname Porgie, but plums never featured again as they chatted for another twenty minutes. Then, with goodbyes, Siman drew the curtains together saying, "We don't want them eavesdropping on our conversations".

They sat outside in the sun, sheltered from the sea breeze by a wall of glass which had the effect of cutting down background noise. Up here it was a different world.

"I can see why you chose this place", ventured George, but not addressing the Smiths by any particular name or title.

"George, do call us Grandma and Grandpa". Janu timed her comment naturally so there was no awkwardness for the young man. "Everybody else does, whether family or not!"

Siman pointed south-east over the rooftops. "You see that light grey roof; that's number 66 King's Road and it's near the fishing museum. Louise and Robert have the corner flat with a great view of the pier. There's always so much going on for them to watch".

Io picked up the thread. "They like their routines and love joining in Church on Sunday mornings. Their sound system is amazing and the camera is positioned where they used to sit. Apart from the occasional head

45

blocking the view it's almost as if you are there".

"So they don't actually go to Church but still feel included. That sounds a bit odd to me", George puzzled.

"No, it works really well. Visitors can call too and join the atmosphere; Sunday mornings have been part of their routine for so many years. Robert was particularly pleased last week because the minister mentioned his question in the sermon, something about pigs rushing into the sea when filled with evil spirits". She paused a moment as the thought occurred to her, "George, would you like to join them?"

"Yes I suppose I would but I've never really been to Church". He didn't feel pressurized by the invitation; in fact he had become quite curious and valued the opportunity to see things for himself.

"That doesn't matter because, like a pub, anyone can walk into the building. The real Church is people anyway, so buildings and communications are all secondary. It's keeping it personal that counts".

They made the necessary change of plan and settled down to a 'light lunch' before heading for a walk along the sea front. Janu and Siman stayed home pottering in the garden as the next meal took shape!

At 9.20am that Sunday Io and George set off from The Penthouse of The Old Broadcasting House as it was now known, and walked past the clock tower down West Street to the front; then east along King's Road and into number 66.

George didn't quite know what to expect; they made their way up the stairs so as to maximise exercise and dissipate some of Janu's calorie contributions. The door opened as they approached and they were immediately welcomed into a different kind of world.

"Do come in and make yourselves at home". As usual Louise led but Robert chipped in, "We chose this place because it looks out to sea and also allows us to snoop on all the pier tourists. You'd be surprised what goes on. A sea view is fantastic but changes slowly and can get a bit boring".

Somehow this introduction summed the elderly couple up. They were welcoming, enjoyed the patterns of life and nature but also wanted the stimulation of watching the world and his wife go by.

"Would you like a cuppa? Tea? Coffee? Bit early for a beer George". Robert organised Louise seamlessly. Soon they were sitting in four comfortable chairs facing some thick velvet curtains. Louise lit a couple of candles and placed a fresh rose at the foot of a simple wooden cross set in an alcove.

"What's the time dear?" asked Louise. "It's quarter to ten, so they will be getting ready". Robert drew the curtains which showed St Paul's Church being prepared for worship. Various members of the choir in their smart blue robes were putting out music sheets. Candles were lit on the altar. Then Robert pushed one of the buttons and the picture faded to another view of a prayer corner with a votive candle stand. There was a font and various flags.

"Oh look, there's Edna, bless her", commented Louise. "She's done well to get to Church; dear old Reginald's funeral was only last Wednesday. I sent her a card Robert".

George was captivated. He felt quite absorbed by

the 'surroundings' and yet was sitting in a flat some distance from the Church. He felt as if he should speak in hushed tones but was assured that, although they could hear sounds, their chatter couldn't be overheard.

"Do drink up George. I'm sure Greatma has another one in the pot", said Io. She made it clear that they could be respectfully part of their Church while at the same time relaxing at home. The congregation stood when the first hymn was announced.

"Oh, I love this one. We can all join in; our neighbours are used to Sunday Church". Louise's voice was rather tremulous, had dropped a little with the years, but fortunately was still fairly accurate. Io sounded amazing. George hadn't heard her sing before. He joined in quietly. Robert had a go but his efforts bore little resemblance to the tune; it was clear that he enjoyed giving it his best shot. The rumble gave an audio cushion beneath which George could be a little more adventurous.

08 House plans

For a number of weeks Silvanus had been thinking carefully; for reasons of security he had never written or typed anything down, but had developed a systematic way of attacking the problem by using different rooms of a house. He turned off all links with sphinx because he was close to making sufficient decisions to put a plan into action. This was an opportunity to clear his mind without anything being detected.

Because he was such a wily character nearly all his relationships with his fellow human beings atrophied so he found his three dogs great companions; they always seemed loyal, they always had a capacity for fun, and they always had energy.

From his cottage in Eriswell Silvanus could be at the Lakenheath Rider Servicing Complex in just seven minutes. But now he was going to pass by the massive site. He checked his eCar was fully charged through its carbon-enriched tyres positioned over the charging pads fitted outside his garage. The dogs wagged their tails crazily and jumped in the back. As they headed along Brandon Road for Thetford Forest he noticed the beauty of winter from the warmth of the car; and the engineer in him also saw that the battery was charging through road contacts. After an unbelievably wet and stormy autumn, he was surprised and delighted by a bright crisp day. It was a relief after all the hectic activity of the previous weeks merely to have time to think.

Silvanus and fitness regimes were poles apart and yet in a way he was a disciplinarian; if he wanted his body to do something it had to respond. Usually it was over-fat and under-exercised but when he had something on his mind he could walk for mile after mile without apparently noticing. It was a long time since he had actually been in fresh air and uncharacteristically he thought that he ought to exercise a little more.

If Silvanus was frustrated the dogs would have commands shouted at them, but today they were virtually ignored and enjoyed ferreting about in the undergrowth while maintaining reasonable progress in order to keep up with him. They walked one of the circuits he knew well so he could lose himself planning; he made a point of being polite and relaxed with anyone he encountered. A gent in tweeds and meticulous beard told him off for not keeping his dogs on a lead but Silvanus didn't respond with his usual temper; not being noticed was the priority.

In his mind's eye Silvanus moved from room to room in the house that was his plan. The garage represented assembling the plan ready to drive it forward; he now knew what he was going to do, he would infiltrate the rider upgrade programme and insert a manned capsule. The bedroom, and unusually for him in this particular house he only had one, represented timing. Silvanus knew he might need to keep his plan sleeping for some time. The key to the whole design made the lounge the place where he had to relax so that everything appeared normal. If the psychological detection programme (run so effectively by Inflow) was to detect any significant change in his behaviour, suspicion and intelligence might lead authorities to his Cell and into the house of his mind. It was a dangerous game.

That night Silvanus slept well and so for that matter did his dogs. The plan crafted so carefully in his mind, room by imaginary room was nearing completion. He would call one full meeting of his Cell, and that would be followed by meetings with individuals. Only he would know the full house plans. The meetings with individuals might in some cases be quite complex, but would only include information required by that particular member. Nothing would be recorded and he would keep the whole atmosphere as relaxed and easy going as possible so that the behaviour of Cell members did not appear to change.

Silvanus knew that he had to be particularly careful with himself because his desire to control and manipulate was going to be satisfied by his plan. The excitement of that possibility surged through his veins. More relaxation was key, so there were more walks in Thetford Forest and Silvanus was surprised by how much he noticed as Nature prepared to paint spring. He pencilled in the idea of walking the cliffs at Cromer; he hadn't been there since childhood.

He got to taking his old binoculars with him and observing wild life; very convenient too because he could act as a twitcher if he did not want recognition. The walks were a help but he still felt the need to slow down further and so he investigated various alternatives including yoga, but all the groups seem to be composed of women; jogging, but that was a solitary exercise designed merely to use up energy; and finally cycling, which caught his imagination.

Silvanus invested in a new road bicycle which he

found surprisingly comfortable to ride and came to enjoy conversations on the bronchs where people talked freely about everything you could imagine. He began to cycle regularly and always with some purpose in mind; that way he felt that it wasn't just using up his energy but harnessing it.

One evening, after a couple of months, as he lay in a bath having a good soaking he chuckled to himself because he realized his ruthlessness had made him physically fitter and slightly lighter.

09 Valuing

"Have you ever been involved in diplomacy, Mr Kimmler?" asked William, his dark eyebrows lifting in a quizzical frown as they walked the quad. Of course Ashley was there too. Gustav encouraged students to walk round and round the metaguild quad as they wrestled with an idea. Exercise brought oxygen to the brain. They were wrapped up warm against the cold, and the frosty air caught their breath.

"Not directly, no; but I have a beach which is dedicated to diplomacy. For years I've been trying to influence the United Nations (UN) to develop a simple Value to Living index. For many animals life is just an existence, and that is sadly true for millions of human beings too. Funnily enough what sparked me off was reading an old copy of a newspaper written when fox hunting was banned last century; someone had compared the lifestyles of different animals. If I remember correctly pigs came off best, chicken worst, and foxes somewhere in between".

Ashley wanted more detail about the Value to Living index. His contact lenses had become uncomfortable so he was wearing glasses and checked them. *Often managers and civil servants seek to measure value added to a function, for example education. The Value to Living index (or V2L) seeks to quantify the whole of a being's lifespan in terms of quality not just quantity. The index allocates scores against seven phases in life, with one additional score for the spiritual component, and is designed to be easily determined.*

Gustav Kimmler responded, "That's right. I remember them from Jacques' soliloquy in As You Like It by William Shakespeare, with one additional score added for the whole span. Let me show you an example". Gustav had real skill in setting out his ideas on an impressive V2L beach that he ran. It used suckling piglets against a rural skyline as the home image. He hoped that, as waves of information broke upon his beach, they would in turn carry his ideas across the world.

He also loved tradition and pulled an ancient fountain pen from his inside jacket pocket and stopped walking so as to write on some card which he propped up on one leg supported by a bench. The lads were fascinated by his dexterity and the way in which he seemed so at ease with such an odd instrument.

"It starts, 'All the world's a stage, and men and women merely players'. Let's take a male free-range pig rather than a person as our first example. How does it begin? Ah yes, 'the infant mewling and puking' is the piglet stage which is well husbanded with little stress except for the tails being cut off, and administration of various vaccines. Let's give it a high score, say 8 out of 10. What's the next phrase?"

Gustav capped the pen and put it with the card inside his jacket, rubbed his hands against the bitter cold and put them in his trouser pockets. They walked on, cheeks aglow.

Ashley loved the quaint rhythm of Shakespeare's style and already had sphinx telling him *the whining school boy, with his satchel and shining morning face* ... Gustav cut in, "Ah yes ... 'unwillingly to school'; that's

54

when piglets run around together and learn their place in the pig village. I think that's another 8. Remember these scores because we'll complete the card in a minute". They walked at a good pace to keep warm.

"Then comes the 'lover, sighing like furnace'; with artificial insemination and castration of most male piglets this stage is a bit tame: 1 out of 10". Gustav paused long enough to write the number on his card. "The soldier's stage 'full of oaths, and bearded like the pard' is more worthwhile, not in fighting terms but in various social groupings established on free range farms. It would be reasonable to argue for 6".

William anticipated Gustav's next thought, "But pigs don't live into old age because they are killed for food". A quizzical look flashed across the dark features of his face. "You're right there; the 'justice' followed by the failing stages with 'big manly voice, turning again towards childish treble' are only seen by the occasional boar kept on as a stud. With modern culling methods the average pig never smells death or has any idea that it is coming. Robots cull only the required pigs almost simultaneously and, when well programmed, discreetly so that other pigs are hardly aware of death; they just wonder where their companions have gone! Pigs don't face the trauma of wasting away and they die in peak condition so I would give 5 out of a possible 20 for these two stages".

"Do you think that humans should be culled too?", asked Ashley shifting his balance as if the thought made him uncomfortable.

"Well, V2L might help. There's no point in existing just for the sake of it; however the elderly are our greatest source of wisdom because they can draw on a sense of perspective. Our pics are set to 110 years after which, if we want medical attention, we have to demonstrate a certain quality of life; otherwise there will be no intervention just to extend life. Let's complete the index for a male pig and then you can calculate something for a human being. Let's tot up the score so far".

They stopped walking and sat down on a convenient bench sheltered from the biting east wind and catching some thin winter sun. Gustav showed them his card which they completed. "Nothing else can be added because life is cut short. 'Sans teeth, sans eyes, sans taste, sans everything' does not apply to pigs. There appears to be no spiritual side to a pig although some say they make good pets; let's be generous and add on 5 points. That gives us a total of 33 out of 80".

stage	male pig
infancy	8
student	8
lover	1
soldier	6
justice	5
2nd childhood	0
oblivion	0
spirit	5

33

"You can see that it's simple to come up with a value, and it gets people talking which puts the whole thing into the public domain, and that's a key feature of V2L. In the early part of this century the World Health Organization (WHO) came up with a Quality of Life scale or WHOQOL for short. It was a fantastic attempt to assess well-being internationally. Unfortunately the research became complex and bogged down by copyright issues, so it never entered into public use".

He paused for questions or comments but was surprised by attentive silence; perhaps it was the cold. Anyway he continued.

"There was an attempt to make it accessible called the 'happiness index' but understandably it was rubbished as 'political correctness gone mad'. You try out V2L for an unwanted child without access to good education, and I think you will begin to see its power".

Ashley began, "The first stage is the mewling puking infant which for an unwanted child is likely to be tough, probably involving physical abuse. I reckon the first five years of life are when children pick up a real feel for what life is about, and to learn that nobody loves you is a hard cross to carry. The score would be low, say 2 out of 10".

"But that's worse than a piglet's start!", cut in Will. "That's the whole point of V2L, it make us think about living as opposed to existing, and it applies to all sentient beings", explained Gustav. "Many human beings have been given dreadful lives". He wrote on his card.

Ashley was curious because he had had to carry a cross himself when his parents divorced. "The whining school boy can't be so bad; the child will feel friendship at school, say 7; that makes a measly 9 so far".

"Hang on a minute", cut in Gustav, "I said this child had no access to good education. I think 7 is too generous; more like 3 because the child could be trapped in a so-called home".

"The lover, sighing like furnace ought to be a good stage with a real sense of being wanted but perhaps finding it difficult to trust, say 7 out of 10. That makes 12 out of 30 and we're catching up on the pig", explained Will with a slight sense of relief. It seemed appalling that an animal should score higher than a human.

"Then comes the soldier full of strange oaths which I suppose is professional life since national service was abolished ages ago", argued Ashley who was a pacifist by nature. "What do you think, Will?"

"It can't be less than 5; sometimes those who have had a difficult upbringing have natural resilience in a competitive market place, how about 8? That gives a cumulative total of 20 and we've nearly caught up the pig if I read your writing correctly Mr Kimmler".

"I think you're beginning to see the power of this idea and why I have dedicated so much time and effort to influencing the swell with my beach". There was a brief pause, which reinforced the sense of Gustav's utter conviction. They considered the justice and, after a long debate about learning from life, came up with a score of 6. The final stages of life gave the most difficulty but they settled for 4 in each, 34 out of 70 so far ... only one more than a male pig! Only the spiritual component could make a difference. They agreed that sometimes disadvantaged people have profound spiritual lives and gave it 7. Gustav showed the card which they noticed had one more column waiting to be filled.

stage	male pig	unwanted human	valued human
infancy	8	2	
student	8	3	
lover	1	7	
soldier	6	8	
justice	5	6	
2nd childhood	0	4	
oblivion	0	4	
spirit	5	7	
	33	41	

10 Interest

"There's nothing here, Ash", summed up Silvanus in an off-handed manner. "What's so interesting about this Gustav man then?" Ashley sighed and replied trying not to let his frustration show. "That's the whole point, father. He is instant with history or wave mechanics or whatever, but it's the background that really counts. Bright waves don't necessarily carry wisdom".

"You and your wisdom! It's almost as if you had a girlfriend called Wisdom". Metaguild did not excite Silvanus; he found the atmosphere rather flat. The buildings were traditional, rather ordinary and gathered in clusters to form quadrangles joined by interconnecting passages. People walked everywhere it seemed. Why all this wasted walking? The open evening was billed as an opportunity for the extended families of freshers to participate in mining wisdom. After welcoming drinks, cheeses of every description, and thin slices of delicious dried fruits, they were ushered into a large new lecture theatre based on a Greek oval auditorium.

The guild master introduced herself by thanking so many who, by supporting their fresher, were also supporting a new dream in education. It was a warm brief speech; its main purpose was to introduce Gustav. He was so ordinary that Silvanus thought it some sort of joke. The lights dimmed slightly. Although this prophet of wisdom had little physical magic his immediate power over the audience was remarkable. How could such an underwhelming man draw his listeners; it was his controlled passion, his conviction, his power of

60

understatement, and the attraction of the challenge he made. Gustav's boyish face, expressive eyebrows and dark complexion were not the norms in a visual communicator; somehow it gave his message more strength.

This man had total confidence in wisdom so long as it was proclaimed accurately. He had come to appreciate his role as a custodian when considering the market value of stand-up comics, and the election of Ron Johnson in 2010 to a seat in the US Senate. The former use few props and often command an empty stage with just a microphone and spotlight. The latter gave a passionate speech about personal liberty, posted it on the ether, and gained such a following that he also gained his place in history.

Gustav and Silvanus could have been from different planets and yet they shared the same dominant feature. Gustav would hound his quarry in order to extract the maximum enrichment it could provide. Silvanus had steel determination to reach his declared goals. Could these two disciples in the arts of ruthless guile ever meet in a shared cause? Only time would tell. They were both charismatic leaders whose influence on a relatively small number of followers could engender enormous change.

Io was very fond of her goddaughter, Pamela who was more introspective by nature but enjoyed the stimuli of 'question' and 'adventure' upon which Io had been nurtured. Pamela had asked Io, whom she considered to be her aunt, to join the family at the metaguild open evening and she had snapped up the opportunity to meet Mr Gustav Kimmler. He didn't disappoint.

Io enjoyed her own space and wasn't a bit perturbed when Pamela joined the chatter of her fellow students. Pamela's proud parents gradually drifted off too as they compared notes with other parents, so Io at last had the chance to wander off and explore a campus which enjoyed investment in beauty as well as technology. It was a college set in an art gallery.

Silvanus had come with his ex, Holly. They were doing their bit as parents but it was obvious why they had parted; there was so little language between them. He was angry at heart, and she was just very shallow. Not an air-head but the loft was rather empty. She had good powers of articulation but these centred on the trivia of the virtual world. The flat screens on her walls were more real than the windows to the garden.

"Who's that stunning girl, Ash?" inquired Silvanus looking across the auditorium in Io's direction. "Who's who?" responded Ashley already wondering why he had to have his father in tow; he seemed completely ignorant as to the ethos of metaguild and why Ashley resonated to its design. The boy felt the scars of his parents' divorce itching; then he had known rejection, and now it all flashed back. His father, the great and powerful Silvanus, just smacked of betrayal. What annoyed Ashley was why he still reacted so; he had chatted to Will about it and even been to see Will's minister, Pete who told him he had the great gift of sensitivity and would have to learn how to use it.

"I'd like to meet her. Come on, let's go over". Ashley responded in such a way that made it obvious that he found Silvanus tiresome, "You go if you want to, father; I'll stay here with my mother". He didn't want to hurt his father because he loved him as a son but neither was he going to be sweetness and light if it didn't ring true. They parted with mutual relief. Silvanus found the formal 'father' a constant harping back to the past as if there could be no forgiveness, and Ashley who longed to have a father-figure around to support his change from boy to man found Silvanus disgusted him.

Io was standing fascinated by a picture; she looked awesome, not through surgery or make up, but because she was so very natural. The picture was an interpretation of a sight she knew too well. The Fish, her work place, had been painted as if planted in the sea. It was true that the Inflow complex was surrounded by a wide moat which somehow visually lifted it above the fenland because the sky reflected around the massive stem. The lake was primarily there for reasons of security, and had been made by opening up the Little Ouse river to form a large expanse of water north of the railway and east of the sluices to the Cut-off Channel; thus water level was easily controlled.

Io was intrigued by the painting's background; it seemed to contain emotion. All that communication was represented in salutations, in passion, in delighted hesitation, in purpose. Quantities of information, of texture, of tone competed with realities of spirit, of hope, of well-being. The more she looked at the picture, the more absorbed she became.

She didn't realize Silvanus had approached. "Hello, my name is Silvanus, you seem to see something in this picture". Io didn't even notice him and carried on looking. So he tried again, "Sorry to interrupt your thoughts, I gather that is your work place. I can't say that I would be intrigued by a picture of my office". Io turned slowly, and looked at him straight in the eyes not saying anything for a moment; how dare he invade her space. With all his energies for control, management and manipulation, he felt strangely challenged by her look. They had never really met before but knew quite a bit about each other through the conversations that spilled around Gustav's pod.

"I suppose", she said, "that Silvanus, the tree-man would have an attitude like that". Silvanus quipped back, "And I suppose Io the moon-maiden would constantly rotate around some boring little planet". They laughed slightly uncomfortably and then Silvanus continued, "Anyway tell me what fascinates you in this picture?"

She began to point out its detail and, as she had so often found, it was during her explanation that she came to understand why she was uneasy in her work at the Fish. So much of what was communicated was little more than entertainment. It was as if all life was just one long episode of a soap opera, without even an intermission! The more the world communicated the less real it became.

This picture was about bringing souls together, about minds comparing their zest for life, about living and not merely existing. But she knew that most of what passed through the Fish was just junk.

11 Disturbance

"Remember that sphinx, buddy and sab should only be used in a real emergency, and that is why they have been sealed. The whole point of this exercise is to throw you back on your own resources". Gustav went through his briefing and then in mid morning dropped his charges east of the river Avon not far from Bath.

There was real excitement in the pod; it was mixed with apprehension. They huddled together in the thin spring sunshine: Pamela Smith, Zoid Shevardnadze, William Inchbald, Ashley Woodlander, and Alfred Cookson. This was the first time in their lives that their comms aids had been disabled. Although they had been over procedures many times it was a bit hairy. Being a Suffolk lad it was also the first time Alfred had seen proper hills!

"We've two days to get to Salisbury Cathedral without being detected. I reckon we should concentrate on finding suitable cover for tonight and then make a really early start in the morning".

Zoid's suggestion went down well; his dark features showed concern. This exercise was going to be a huge challenge because his ear and eye implants had been turned off giving him a sense of disorientation coupled with a mild headache. He had to rely on others who normally wore glasses, contact lenses, and ear grommets.

Soon the team were pouring over old paper Ordinance Survey maps. Pamela had remembered something about Box Hill rail tunnel being used for weapon storage during the Second World War. A train would enter the tunnel and soon afterwards a similar train would leave the other end allowing the original to unload freight. The area was riddled with underground networks.

After the war some had been used for growing mushrooms. The largest was Monkton Farleigh Mine which consisted of 80 acres of tunnels and storage districts, with air shafts secluded beneath trees, and the remains of an old air conditioning power plant still around. The hunt was on to find a suitable tunnel entrance and therefore shelter from any monitoring riders detecting heat.

It all took longer than they thought it might. Crossing the river was easy once they found the canal; the towpath made for good speed and soon they were on the aqueduct which took them above river and railway. From there they walked north along the east bank of the Avon until climbing diagonally up the hill to Brown's Folly. The woodland was awash with primroses. They were on the outskirts of Monkton Farleigh village and soon some shafts were discovered. Trying not to show her concern Pamela volunteered, "It's a bit creepy in here".

"At least it's dry and doesn't seem to smell too much", said William in a slightly over-confident tone.

Good old baked beans, almost indestructible; they even managed to get them warm and make a decent cup of tea. Tinned rice pudding closed a very basic supper as the group chatted away merrily; it had been a good start towards Salisbury. Their confidence was high; even though their comm's umbilical cords had been cut they had still achieved much.

Chatter ebbed away as tiredness took over. Excitement didn't make sleep easy, and as they quietened so the natural noise of the countryside entertained them. An owl sharing their shelter screeched. The pod's confidence wavered.

As ears tuned-in to this new soundscape all became aware of a distant regular breathing which was slow and easy and deep. What on earth could be making such soothing, disturbing sounds?

Frightened whispers broke out. Ashley asked everyone to keep really quiet so they could concentrate on identifying the sound. After some debate the pod decided to tie a rope between two rucksacks loaded with cooking gear to provide a trip wire and alarm down the tunnel in case anything came towards them. Each would then take a turn to keep watch and note any changes in the sound pattern. In the morning the tunnel would be investigated. The steady rhythm of the slow breathing didn't change and after the day's exercise the group were soon all asleep, including Zoid who had volunteered first watch.

Ashley was awake first and decided to set off the trip wire; his companions were petrified. Their noise increased until the obvious was pointed out that, if they could hear the breathing, it might hear them. What made such a natural unnerving sound?

Pamela found herself, to the surprised of the others, taking a lead. She agreed to break the seal on her sab, not to transmit but to take flash pictures looking back at every junction so they could retrace their steps. She also used its light once away from the entrance.

The underground network was surprisingly dry since water naturally drained down through the limestone and they were many metres above the river Avon. It may also have been that the ground was warm; after all, the hot water springs of Bath were not that far away. The pod travelled along tunnels heading towards the breathing. Ahead light began to spill over the ceiling; it seemed so bright.

They had agreed not to speak and to avoid surveillance cameras if at all possible. Very slowly they approached the light coming up from a grating in the floor. The breathing was so close it was almost as if they were inside the mouth of some enormous creature. One by one they became aware that a trickle of air was being drawn through the grating; they were in some kind of fresh air supply duct. Any noise would carry into the chamber below.

Regular deep slow breathing was complemented by the hum of machinery and by a video screen. Pamela was the first to ease her head over the grating; the others could see her eyes widening in a mix of awe, curiosity, horror, and anger. The others took turns. All were traumatised by the scene. Confident Zoid's eyes filled with silent tears. They had to tell others.

Salisbury was reached in good time. The metaguild students felt they needed to enter the cathedral; it wasn't something they could articulate but forgiveness was part of it, not for what they had done but for what they had seen. Lighting votive candles helped. The beauty of Evensong seemed both distant and irrelevant, and yet it provided balm for their souls.

Afterwards kindly old stewards chatted to them; they felt welcomed and appreciated. They had to talk to Gustav. Pamela had to talk to Io.

12 Purpose

Of course nowhere was completely safe from surveillance but there was a kind of unwritten agreement that the bronchs should be kept as free as possible. These codes were broken by those insensitive to tradition, and of course issues of national security recognize no boundaries. Generally speaking the understanding worked well but it was unclear quite how it had evolved.

Why was it for instance that in New Zealand celebrities could freely walk around Queenstown, but be pursued by media hunters in Auckland? Perhaps it was because true New Zealand 'Southern men' were more interested in sheep production than superstars. When they gathered in their outback taverns for a handle of ale the conversation rarely turned to the plastic world of soft lenses and hype, rather it would focus on the real world of the weather patterns, rugby games, and, in the depths of winter, curling. Their North Island counterparts on the other hand were altogether more attuned to pink.

Io and George simply enjoyed the freedom on the bronchs. Their friendship had grown through easy conversation. George felt free to talk without reserve about his family and in particular Basil. It helped him immensely to get a different perspective on things. The Freeman family had had to find a way of coping; now Io's wisdom and careful listening helped him move towards a better understanding and possible review of their decision that Basil live in a hostel. It had given him some independence but it was clear that he was so unhappy and longed to be more useful.

George was grateful. "I still remember your amazing moonlit beauty the first time I saw you. I knew then that you were exceptional, but I never imagined that I would receive such wonderful wise counsel. Thank you".

In turn she began to express her unease about Inflow. "You see, I've been ill at ease for some time. It's not about Inflow mechanisms or personnel; no it's more about purpose. You're helping me reflect".

George reassured her, "I've no security concerns. It was a great relief to write those out soon after I got to know you. My job is over because your behaviour only shows mild unease; you still work incredibly efficiently. My real worry is that my behaviour might be detected and give our friendship away".

"So relax then!" Io teased him gently and fondly, "Let me monitor you for a change!" She paused and looked at him, leaning her head slightly to one side. "George, what's the point of all this mass of information flowing about?"

"Never really thought about it. I suppose it's a bit like producing electricity; you don't know how people will use it, you just generate it in the cheapest, cleanest way. It's up to others to sort out what's right and wrong, what's useful or wasteful. You can't send good electricity to some houses but refuse others!"

"George, I need purpose". He lifted his left arm from his handlebar to pat her shoulder, and asked, "Why?"

"Well, what's the point in life if you just drift along without making a difference?" Their bikes moved smoothly as they headed beside the railway to Lakenheath. Spring growth was turning the fens into its massively productive stage where fields several miles wide yielded vast quantities of tasteless carrots, onions, and the like. But Io and George were too absorbed to notice.

"Can't your lifestyle make a difference? You make a difference to me". Io knew then that she needed a cause not just a lifestyle.

"George, I'm going down to Weymouth next week-end to see Mum and Dad; would you like to join me? The weather forecast is good so we might get a proper walk along the cliffs. I need to do some thinking". George was delighted with invitation.

They went their separate ways as the fronds of the huge land-based jellyfish invited them into its world. Another working day 'monitoring behaviour' for George, and 'making information flow quicker and more naturally' for Io.

Everything smelt fresh as Spring played her Symphony in Green; the subtlety of shades played in the early morning sun as the train sped towards Cambridge. For several miles it was completely flat and completely straight, with level crossings every few minutes. A gentle curve took them past Waterbeach and Io caught a fleeting glimpse of the metaguild campus. She had been intrigued by Gustav Kimmler's introduction and puzzled by Silvanus' introduction of himself.

As Baits Bite Lock flashed by on her left the train began to slow for Cambridge station where George joined her. His new thermos was soon providing fresh red bush tea. They chatted about the spires of the famous city, its superb views of the Backs of the colleges east of the river Cam.

By the second cup of tea the thin outskirts of London began to increase in density as the train neared Liverpool Street station; buildings seemed to be piled on top of the terminus. They picked up bikes from the platform racks and cycled up a gentle slope into the bronchs. Io loved this section because it had so much variety.

Firstly they went south along Cycle Super-highway 1 which took up half of the old A3 road. When they reached the Thames river they headed west inside the Blackfriars bronch. It was low tide as they sped under three bridges well above the waterline. At high tide the bronch would be submerged.

Before Victoria Embankment they forked gently left and descended in the diagonal tunnel beneath the river Thames and then up and out on the South Bank. Soon they were opposite the Palace of Westminster where Big Ben gleamed in the spring sun. In a few minutes and after cycling beneath six bridges, they had reached Battersea Park, where they took a diagonal and high flyover section to the correct platform for the Weymouth train at Clapham Junction station.

More tea, this time from Io's flask. They had picked up a bite to eat at the station. London eventually thinned out for the rolling chalk-land of Surrey. This section was reasonably fast and the ride comfortable, George had a brief nap while Io read. At Southampton the train divided leaving the rear five coaches to become a slow stopping train to Bournemouth. Their front section stopped only once at Brockenhurst for the Isle of Wight branch line.

Dorset seemed to slow everything down as the track skirted around Poole Harbour. The train stopped more frequently including Winfrith Research Park where a dozen excited young engineers joined. Io told George she was pleased to see them because her father worked from the site and had campaigned for a request halt with a carriage length platform. After Dorchester South and the Ridgeway Tunnel they were met at Upwey station by Io's parents, Claru and Arthor Smith.

Io breathed in the fresh sea air and for a brief moment felt homesick. No bronchs were needed here; the gentle hills hugged Weymouth Bay, Portland and Chesil Beach. Mum and Dad hugged their daughter but did not embarrass George with too intimate a greeting. Arthor gave him a pat on the shoulder and said, "Welcome George. It is great to see you for real after all the glimpses through our family windows".

"Thanks. I'm ashamed to say I've never been to Dorset before, but it has already impressed me. Isn't this where the Olympic sailing took place back in 2012?" There was an easiness in his tone; after all he had already met great and grand parents in Brighton. It was intriguing to see various family traits passed down from one generation to another. There was no pretence in this clan.

"Remember George that time travels slower here. We still don't have a motorway and many pass us by as they head for Devon and Cornwall". He unhooked his trailer bike and adjusted the saddle for George. Io and Claru had already cycled underneath the railway and along cycle tracks to the Engine Estate as it was known. George and Arthor soon caught them up, and even managed to cycle up Brunel Drive.

"What magnificent views across the bay ... with Portland and the port". George was fit but the last pull had taken some of his breath away.

"Yes, we're truly blessed. In one turn of the head you can see the white cliffs of the Nothe, the sands of Weymouth beach, and the rock of Portland. We hope to walk some of that after coffee". Arthor cycled wherever he could. His naturally curly head of black hair acted as a cushion inside the cycle helmet which he had worn for many a mile. After all his wife Claru was an administrator at their Healthy Neighbourhood office, so he had to do her bidding! Actually, he had come to love purposeful exercise and the opportunity it gave to taste, feel, smell, hear and see Nature's handiwork. Weymouth spring was two weeks ahead of that in the Fens.

Io had asked her parents if she and George could stay the weekend and go for a long walk along the coast. Claru and Arthor had loaded two fisherman's rucksacks which included folding seats. He had learnt from previous conversations with George that he enjoyed traditional ales, and so took him to one side.

"I've managed to smuggle in some Butcombe Brunel bitter for us to enjoy; after all you can't be booked for drunkenly driving a rucksack!" George was intrigued by Io's father because he had a warm playfulness but clearly showed important strategic insight!

"Why is this called the Engine Estate? Obviously Brunel is famous for the Great Western Railway, early bridges and ships; but what about Churchward, Wainwright and Stanier that we cycled past on the way?"

"I must say you are very observant". George wondered for a moment if his well honed surveillance skills might have given him away, but Arthor continued. "They were all designers of steam engines. You see the Southern Railway was the last to be electrified, and so any engines still serviceable were sent here; Weymouth has seen virtually every model. Someone with some imagination decided to use the names on the local roads".

They set off on bikes via the delightfully named Puddledock Lane, through Sutton Poyntz and along the White Horse Valley cycle path. The weather forecast proved right. Even though it was spring the sun was almost too hot; however when they had been through Osmington and down to the Mills a sea breeze greeted them. They locked up their bikes and hid them behind a hedge. It was good exercise walking up the coastal path to Holworth.

"Oh George, come and look at St Catherine's Chapel", invited Io. He was surprised to find something akin to a large black garden shed perched above the cliffs. On closer inspection the place had real character and a sense of peace. He had joined Io's grandparents in satellite Church, and now he found a place that spoke to him.

Claru and Arthor had entered unnoticed and there fell a natural silence, Io sat on a simple chair while George walked quietly around soaking up the atmosphere and detail. An etched window in memory of a past minister teased his focus; one minute he looked straight through it to the trees behind, the next a picture of a chapel stood out clearly against a mixed green background.

When he turned around Io was kneeling at the rail with tears running down her face. He felt it appropriate to respect her privacy rather than offer comfort, partly because that is exactly what her parents did. Somehow here in this thin place, where the worlds of heaven and earth were comfortable with each other, it was appropriate; it was a kind of wordless prayer of immense power, both expressive and receptive.

George saw Io's face had something from her mother's features. It was plain country beauty that needed no paint or plaster. He was moved to say a prayer, but which? Quietly he moved his lips to the Lord's Prayer, "Our Father, who art in heaven ... on earth as it is in heaven ..." There was a resonance for him in that second phrase.

After a while Io dried her eyes, gave her nose an unseemly noisy blow and effectively announced it was time to carry on walking. They all knew that when ready she would talk of a simple prayer asking for a cause and not just a lifestyle.

13 Frustration

For two years Charles had watched riders glistening in the morning sun and loafing off into the sky. The updating programme was continuous; every day (as long as winds were not too strong) a rider would land in the cool of the evening and disappear into an underground hanger. During the night the old hardware would be replaced with new modules; hydrogen and oxygen tanks would be refilled; and routine maintenance carried out so that the updated rider could be ready for sunrise and another six months or so drifting in the stratosphere.

There was an ethereal beauty about the riders. Their enormous profile seemed sculptured to please the aesthetic eye even though their design was entirely functional. Matt black titanium skin made their huge bulk blend with any background, and yet when one flew low overhead it was like a thundercloud. Once high enough the rider's shadow became diffuse. Charles was captivated but his real mission wasn't to be fascinated, but to work out a way to subterfuge the rider programme so that Silvanus could hold the information world to ransom.

International convention allowed any sovereign state to launch its own riders so long as it conformed with the Even Space Protocol or ESP. This meant that riders adjusted their floating position to be of equal distance from neighbours and at the same height. Thus no rider would crowd or overshadow others; it also meant that an even positioning gave equal information access and coverage. The convention had worked well for a number of years and there had been no collisions or information blackouts. Each rider servicing facility was positioned away from airports and given well defined flight corridors for take-off and landing. Riders floated well above conventional aircraft altitude.

Charles thought that this protocol could also be a weakness, but how could Silvanus break into it? Hijacking a single rider was useless because information would merely be re-routed via its neighbours. The massive Iceland volcano eruption which took out a rider overhead hardly made any difference to information flow because adjacent riders compensated by adjusting their floating positions. ESP was robust and flexible.

Silvanus had already asked Charles to develop ways of hacking into world-wide channels of communication and he already knew how to do that, but finding access to ESP had proved impossible. He would talk it over with Silvanus. There was an opportunity that evening because the cell had been summoned to gather at The Five Miles From Anywhere hostelry. He watched the newly serviced rider slowly gain height over Mildenhall Fen as it disappeared into the distance. For a moment Charles imagined a Roman soldier looking up into the sky in awe of the site, and then burying his treasure for safety. After all it was in these parts that a Suffolk farmer many years later had unearthed such a treasure. Charles was tired after his watch and so packed his plane-spotting gear into the boot of his little Ford eCar, headed briefly up the A11 to turn left across Wangford Fen, down the B1112, and into Lakenheath town to his home opposite the church. He had a quick breakfast and was soon asleep.

The alarm woke him ready for a shower, a complete change of clothes, and another snack. The eCar had recharged so he drove the county lanes through Beck Row, West Row, Freckenham, and so on, to the Five at Upware. Yes it was slower but Charles felt at home in the open spaces and character of Suffolk.

Victor was the last to arrive and casually chatted to some regulars at the bar; the place was buzzing. After a while he made for the gents, and followed instructions scribbled on a scrap of paper that had been screwed up in his pocket. The snug was an artificial world without any source of natural light. Nobody could quite work out where it was, or exactly how they found it. The entrance usually appeared after travelling down various corridors and intersections all looking exactly the same.

Each person had to follow a simple code: 'G' meant turn right, 'R' left, 'W' straight ahead; any sailor could follow it. If an item of shopping had a qualifying phrase he had to take notice of the first letter, if not he should ignore it. On successful entry to the snug he had to eat the list!

1) *butter*	ignored
2) *cheese*	ignored
3) *a bunch*	the 'g' told him 'right' to the far
of red grapes	cubicle; Victor locked the door; another door opened in the wall; he pulled the flush and closed the hidden door behind him; the cubicle door unlocked
4) *walnuts*	ignored

5) a box of	the 'w' told him 'ahead' at the
red wine	junction of corridors, all of which were
	painted matt white
6) cold sliced	the 'g' led to another hidden door on
gammon	right which opened as he lent against
	the wall, and this revealed the snug.

Silvanus was angry. At one level nobody knew what Silvanus was thinking; in terms of plans, he kept things close to his chest. In fact Silvanus' cell didn't really understand what he was on about most of the time. True, they had very specific tasks to complete but couldn't see how they fitted into a coherent plan; and of course, that's just how Silvanus wanted it! But they all knew he was angry and therefore dangerous.

He transmitted some useless information about an allied plot to bomb some distant stadium but not a dickie bird flickered on the ether. That showed communication was blocked. In this dreadful snug they could speak freely.

"Right, let's get to the heart of it. I need to know how rider protocols were set up. Let me concentrate on one area, security. Has anyone any idea how the pattern works?" ... There was dead silence. All knew that a flippant remark might trigger a violent episode. After what had happened to Victor, whose neck implant had been switched on and off again, nobody wanted early rigor mortis. "Well! ... has nobody any ideas? You useless bunch of shite!"

They looked around at each other, trying to egg somebody else on. What was for certain is that a silent response to Silvanus would only inflame his rage. "I'm not sure ..." ventured Victor, but he was cut off by Silvanus.

"Well, keep your ruddy mouth shut then!" There was a brief pause. "I'm not sure", Victor gently repeated, "that the answer is in the cell. We ought to think about our contacts".

Surprisingly, Silvanus took on board the idea. He was desperately hungry to find the key to rider subterfuge. Everything else in his plan was in place. The imaginary house, in which every room contained parts of the scheme, was furnished except for this ESP business. "Ok. I like it. Who are our useful contacts then?"

"Don't look at me honey", piped up Jeanette. Silvanus wasn't going to anyway. His girlfriend was generally useless when it came to insight, however occasionally her angle on something was so different that it opened up new ideas.

The conversation went on and a noticeable ease descended on the cell. Montague felt his golf club associates, mostly in the nineteenth hole, would yield little. Years ago he had given way to his son's remarkable energy for scheming. A mixture of pride and shame filled his heart; pride at Silvanus powers, and shame that he felt somewhat inadequate in comparison.

Charles didn't come up with much and was also careful not to get too involved in detail because Silvanus had warned him not to give anything away about rider technology. So it was left up to good old reliable Victor to come up with an idea. "Your Ashley is always thinking outside the box and constantly goes on about that Kimmler fellow ..."

"He's a waste of space. Always playing about with history, and aesthetics, and maths, and invention, and ... you name it. But he's never done a decent day's work in his life". Awkwardness enveloped the cell again; it fell silent. Silvanus was like a volcano; was his simmering anger merely a rumble of warning, or would he blow his top?

Passion was tempered by strategic insight. He knew he had been given wise counsel, and he knew he was in a bottleneck. If the ESP issue could be resolved then Silvanus could put his plan into action. Charles was tempted to speak about the protocol but thought he should wait until others had drifted away. In fact both of them wanted the conversation, so Silvanus eased back his anger and actually thanked his cell for coming to the Five; others left until the two were alone.

"Silvanus, the Even Space Protocol is key. I've tried thinking about it from so many different angles but can't work out a way to invade the codes. Each time I come back to the same thing; there must be a simple gate into the software, but I'm blowed if I can find it".

Charles' words were confirmation for Silvanus that, despite of all his natural instincts, he needed to tap Gustav Kimmler for wisdom. This could be part of his discipline because it was essential that no trait in his behaviour gave away his greater plan to hold the communication flows of Northern Europe in his grip.

14 Distortion

When Pamela shared her worries with Io about what the pod had seen in Monkton Farleigh Mine it united them in a cause that would reveal itself as they walked forward – together. "Please come with me; my friends are great but don't have your wisdom, they don't understand me like you do".

Io gladly accepted; could this be the purpose she craved? Perhaps one day she would have the privilege of her own children but now she had a growing bond with Pamela. "What about inviting Mum and Dad along too?" she asked, not so much expecting a positive response as making sure she didn't overstep into parental responsibilities.

Pamela was quite clear she didn't want her parents there, neither was Io acting in loco parentis. No, here was a parallel relationship of deep value in its own right. In a few years Pamela would be a mature adult and, as she gently changed from girl to woman, Io respected her attitude. Maturity was not merely a function of age. Io was a friend as well as a godmother.

Rather than risk being seen near the tunnel entrance the pair went without torches, just using moonlight. Their eyes adjusted and even picked out a myriad of primrose flowers which mirrored a constellation. It was for a moment as if an African night sky carpeted the floor. Io stumbled on a boulder but Pamela's hand steadied her. Partly because of the pictures she had previously taken, Pamela knew exactly where they were.

There was no wind. Distant sounds of owls and foxes spoke of nocturnal activity. Every breaking twig seemed too loud. Io froze to the spot. "What was that?" she whispered in Pamela's ear. Because she had never heard the sound before, Io was more scared than her young goddaughter! "That's the sound which freaked us out. That's why we had to explore the tunnel. We're here now".

They entered carefully and Pamela switched on her sab's light which was initially too intense. After a few minutes the light shining up from the grating onto the tunnel ceiling was sufficient and she extinguished her light. The slow natural breathing drew them in; too slow, too deep, too regular. Pamela glanced through the grating and motioned Io to the light.

The udder was like a lake. The back legs were vestigial. The cow (if you could call it that) lay on its back. A tube carried away dung to a methane fermentation vessel. Urine was piped away. Six teat cups gently siphoned away milk. Io's eyes widened with terror; it was as if the animal was being raped. She saw as it were a hill beside the milk lake; its slopes rippled gently as the muscles of four enormous stomachs moved food through various stages of digestion. The cow fed from a large teat as a perfect mix of pulped silage, water, and trace elements kept the huge beast's hunger at bay. The chamber was cooled to prevent the cow overheating.

Suddenly the animal was rolled gently on one side. Her back was massaged; a section was washed, dried, and brushed. All the time the pipes conveyed the liquid cargo. Io studied the cow's head which seemed small compared to her enormous bulk. The nostrils were enlarged, the eyes were closed. "Oh Daisy, what have they done to you?" she whispered under her breath.

The cow opened her eyes, flicked her head to disengage the feeding teat, looked straight at Io and let out a low mournful bellow that cut deep into the comely maiden's soul. She burst into tears of revulsion, of raw anger, of deep sadness that her species should so deform another. Here was something wrong ... but why? If nature created the queen bee to be an egg factory wasn't there some sense in helping nature produce a milk factory? Ok, the scale was different; cows aren't insects. The question seemed puerile against her instinctive revulsion. The innocent Io felt polluted. Pamela held her hand tightly.

"It's important we collect evidence. Would you mind holding my rucksack?" Io obliged and Pamela retrieved an extending arm which she screwed onto her sab; she set it to record but was careful to make sure the sab produced no light. As she lowered the device slowly through the grating there was a change of noises below. They wondered if it had triggered an alarm. The cow had stopped eating; cups were more active in draining milk; waste pipes disconnected; and then the bed she was on began to move, it was on rails.

Daisy disappeared slowly down the chamber and began lowing ... to other cows in some meeting place. A young man in white overalls and cap checked the bay where Daisy had lain. A rodent trap was inspected and yielded a large dead brown rat. Equipment was given a quick clean and the man left. Fortunately his cap shielded the sab from view, and in turn his face from the recording.

The mooing conversation changed and soon Daisy's bed returned, but the animal on it was smaller! Markings were exactly the same. The equipment automatically adjusted its plumbing and connected to the younger clone. Soon feed was flowing with the inevitable bi-products.

They hurried out the way they had come in but were careful not to make any noise. Escape was easy; it was the horror of distorted distended Daisy that introduced a sense of panic. Pamela was cool under pressure and stopped to check that the recording had come out; she was very pleased with the result but ensured it wasn't transmitted anywhere. For backup she sent it to Io's sab which also held it securely from the ether. They emerged into the moonlight which bathed them both.

Io wanted to wash herself as if that could take away the contamination in her mind. She wanted to be reassured, to be hugged. Oh, why was the world so cruel, so vicious? Greed, power, lust destroyed beauty and freedom. Could she do something? God help us!

Pamela packed her rucksack carefully, laid it on the ground, relaxed, and let out a great sigh which evolved into sobs. They hugged each other deeply, desperately, mutually reassuring in a shared cause. 'Question' and 'adventure' were their parents.

How the conversion began Io could never explain. In that torture chamber she discovered a new dimension; suddenly a power, a spirit flushed her being through with conviction. She felt baptized in this spirit, was caught up in greater events, and knew a warmth within her which had in it the breath of eternity. A chuckle tickled her throat, and then a shout of pure joy; Pamela joined in a dance of two innocent nymphs.

The snake wiggled.

15 Consultations

Whilst Ashley constantly waxed lyrical about Mr Kimmler's teaching methods he did backup his enthusiasm with facts. Gustav made history live because, with information from sphinx and his critical analysis, it explained contemporary life. He constantly challenged students to think about the vast quantity of information rather than be entertained by its brilliance.

However Ashley was surprised when his father Silvanus sought an appointment with Gustav. "How can I get to see him privately? There's something I want to discuss without nosey busybodies getting involved".

Ashley was suspicious. "He doesn't usually do 'private', father". Silvanus was again annoyed by 'father'; why couldn't Ash grow up and acknowledge him? 'Dad' would mean so much. He was also annoyed by 'private'.

"Why not? Surely people need to talk in private sometimes".

Ashley sighed lightly before answering. "He believes that wisdom is something that belongs to everybody. Those who keep control erode wisdom".

"Ok, but what about commercial secrets? Should a company do all their costly research only for someone else to pinch their ideas and make money?" They debated until Silvanus returned to his quest for an appointment with Gustav Kimmler. Ashley eventually agreed that he would ask that afternoon.

"Thanks, Ash. Much appreciated". Silvanus gave him a quick shoulder-to-shoulder hug. Ashley wondered if it was genuine affection or because his father had just got what he wanted.

"Thanks for seeing me, Mr Kimmler; you're a busy man". Reluctantly Gustav had agreed to meet him in a small study-bay away from the others.

"That's kind of you to say so, but I expect you are busy too. You should certainly take pride that your son Ashley has a fertile mind tempered by a good dose of wisdom. In fact he seems quite a rounded individ...", but Gustav was cut off by Silvanus, who felt flattered and thought it right to take some praise. He reiterated Ashley's superior behaviour. "He's a gifted lad and it's been a pleasure to watch him grow up".

They were both curious as to what made the other tick. Gustav wondered what Silvanus actually did, both in general and particularly in terms of Ashley's development.

There was a brief pause before Silvanus took the initiative. "You have a reputation for history and how it explains our behaviour today. I'll come straight to the point; it's to do with rider evolution. You see I'm interested in developing the next generation which could stay in position for years rather than months".

"I see", puzzled Gustav slowly. "If you have all that technical and I assume entrepreneurial skill why do you think I have anything to offer?"

"You know about ESP?" queried Silvanus raising his pitch towards the end of the question. Could this metaguild boffin have his feet on the ground?

"Yes ... yes I do. 'Even Space Protocol'. In fact it's a key part of my input for freshers. The risk is that they take the rider network for granted just like a previous generation took geostationary satellites for granted".

Silvanus was quite taken in by the easy conversation which nevertheless challenged a bland acceptance of the status quo. Here was a man uncomfortable with institution even though he was a key figure within one. He had that rare gift of being on the inside but being able to look in from the outside. Perhaps history wasn't such a waste of time after all.

"How did ESP begin, and who controls the access? Everything is deeply encrypted to block hackers". Was Silvanus a little too direct he wondered.

"As I understand it the United Nations, in conjunction with both international security agencies and open fair-trade voices, worked up the idea so anybody could take part in the rider scheme. Roughly half the units are sponsored by states, and the other half by global business".

"Ok, I see. So the UN controls access?" Could it be possible that Gustav had provided the key? Silvanus reined in his emotions tightly so as not to create suspicion.

"The collective desire was to encourage as many riders as possible because that would tighten the robustness of communication", explained Gustav.

It was so blindingly obvious. Silvanus had been trying to discover well hidden information about ESP when all the time it was actually an open access protocol provided by the UN. How could he have been so dumb? He would get the codes and challenge the Spaniel to work out a way in.

Gustav remained puzzled by Silvanus who

appeared a personable individual but one hiding so much beneath the surface. Was he actually just another hacker? They parted on good terms and Gustav returned to his study.

He made a mug of red bush tea and sat in his favourite tatty old leather armchair. It held him as if in swaddling bands as he sunk into its comfort. An arm occasionally reached out for the mug. He had exactly 25 minutes catnap, and then stood up, stretched himself by pulling up on a bar across his door, and found his mind refreshingly alert.

The pod appeared a little more animated than usual, which was saying something since their 'cruise control' was statically charged to say the least! Gustav knew he would savour their curious minds; no doubt they had seen something new for the first time, or had a question when the answer was right in front of them. Something was different.

Pamela kept her conversation and second trip to Monkton Farleigh Mine with Io to herself. It wasn't that being the only female in the pod made her in any way uncomfortable; it was that she felt Io was a key to action rather than evaluation.

She maintained her lead of the pod but invited others to paint the picture: a tunnel for shelter, banter and settling down for the night, the deep, slow breathing chilling their minds, guards on duty ... and then a description of the genetically modified cow. She didn't produce eggs like a queen bee, and the worker bees had been replaced by a 'caring' machine; nevertheless humans had 'copied' nature. Two queens, one of eggs and the hives' future; the other of milk, methane, and an entire life in a mine.

They explained how the two seemed morally to be the same and yet how the cow-queen disturbed them very deeply. Why? Before they got to that Zoid suggested they call her gCow, in the style of eCar and so on, because to call her a true cow was incorrect and collusive.

Gustav suggested Ashley and William recall a previous conversation the three of them had had not many weeks before. "Remember the seven ages of man ..."

Ashley duly kicked in, "All the world's a stage, and men and women merely players ... comes from Shakespeare. It gives stages we go through in life. The Value to Living index, or V2L, evaluates each stage out of 10; the total gives the real worth of living".

"Haven't you forgotten something? We added an extra evaluation for the spiritual side of life; the maximum score is 80. If you remember we worked up the V2L for a free-range male pig, and an unwanted human"

Ashley scrabbled around in his pocket and pulled out a crumpled piece of card which he unfolded. "They came to 33 and 41! And, if you remember Mr Kimmler you left one more column for Will and me to fill. It kept us chatting for hours".

The group nodded their heads as if that was to be expected anyway. William took over, "Our main debate was about the failing stages, and how spiritual they could be. Anyway, here's what we came up with". They read out the final line.

stage	male pig	unwanted human	valued human
infancy	8	2	9
student	8	3	9
lover	1	7	8
soldier	6	8	8
justice	5	6	8
2nd childhood	0	4	6
oblivion	0	4	6
spirit	5	7	8
	33	41	62

The pair recalled how much difference valuing human beings made to their lives. Soon the pod were working out V2L for a male pig, queen bee, and gCow. Pamela proudly pulled out her fountain pen and recorded the scores after the pod had debated each stage. They also found the closing stages and spiritual evaluation difficult. What they did appreciate though was the chance for open honest debate.

The result was stark and horrific! There had been much talk trying to evaluate the spiritual life of a queen bee; even if she represented the mind of the hive, she was also an egg factory. The pod felt affirmed in their revulsion on seeing gCow. With wide errors it was still true that her 'life' was worth far less than that of a pig. William couldn't help reflecting that the queen bee fared better than an unwanted child, unless the child's spiritual life was totally fulfilled.

stage	male pig	queen bee	gCow
infancy	8	8	3
student	8	9	3
lover	1	5	0
soldier	6	5	2
justice	5	4	2
2nd childhood	0	4	2
oblivion	0	4	2
spirit	5	6	1
	33	45	15

They left Gustav. What a contrast? Silvanus, a man out to exploit something, possibly to reduce the V2L for those concerned; and the pod, who saw the power of the idea. They wanted to make a difference ... and perhaps they would. He had been impressed by Pamela.

Should Gustav be more proactive in supporting those who boosted V2L for any sentient being? Was his calling just to impart the knowledge base and leave responsibility for action with them, or should he have a just cause? If so, what, how, when? He felt profoundly challenged and decided it was time to take a walk. Perhaps he should buy a bike and get out more!

16 Twilights

Robert woke as his bladder signalled it was time for a short walk. He had dreamed well of past adventures which would now be well beyond the scope of his frail mortal coil. What a fag; but he could almost do the trip in his sleep. The floor was cold. Where were his slippers? Never mind ...

The pain in his leg made him gasp and his breathing was tight; how undignified to be sprawled on the bathroom floor. He had found his slippers alright; the smallest trip and balance was gone. Fortunately he hadn't banged his head, why didn't he take his stick? Too late now. He felt cold.

"Louise!" He tried to shout but couldn't produce much volume. His wife was dead to the world and snored with the angels! Never mind, they should be here soon. It was cold on the floor ... Should have worn his dressing gown; should have taken more care; should have ...

Last time he slowly crumpled to the floor, and afterwards sported impressive bruises for a week or two. But this time the pain ... and cold!

"Siman, Siman, wake up; it's the alarm. Greatpa is in the bathroom and hasn't moved". They dressed by pulling clothes on over their nightwear, and were soon in the car heading towards 66 King's Road. The sea was rough. The door opened as their pics were recognised. Good to be out of the wind. All that noise!

"Quickly, quickly Siman", Janu urged, but he told

her not to panic or one of them might have an accident too. "You don't understand, Dad's so frail!" Siman did but knew Janu needed to express her worrying emotion.

They found Robert on the floor drifting in and out of consciousness. Siman had already called the ambulance and made sure doors were open and emergency guiding lights were on. Louise was still snoring; good because they didn't have to worry about her as well.

"We had better not move him. Oh, bless him, he's so cold. Let's gently cover him with his dressing gown", said Janu, whose rational responses were beginning to temper her emotional ones. She talked reassuringly to her father who let out a shallow groan; perhaps her hand gently caressing his had transferred a loving signal.

In quiet conversation they agreed that Siman would stay with Louise so she wasn't shocked by suddenly facing traumatic news. Janu would go with her father to the hospital.

It was a Friday morning and so, down in Dorset, Arthor and Clairu would be working their normal hours. They only occasionally used the family window in the morning but always drew the curtains just in case. This time Siman looked through. "I thought I should tell you that Janu is in hospital ..."

"Oh dear, what's happened?" You could hear the worry in Clairu's voice. Although working in the Healthy Neighbourhood Centre and being used to urgent calls it was different when it was your own family.

Siman carried on to complete the sentence. "Mum is in hospital with Robert, who had a fall last night. He has broken the head of his femur and is in quite some pain but his pic has a few more years to run so they should operate later this morning".

He remained calm and gave the information, but then added, "Mum got into a bit of a panic but has settled down now". They discussed various options, and agreed that Arthor and Clairu travel to Brighton for the weekend to help everyone develop what would be a new routine.

Siman's gentle but sensitive matter-of-fact style was entirely appropriate as he imparted the news to Louise when she woke. She shared the same approach and there was a good chemistry between them.

"I wonder which of us will die first? I suppose the ideal is that we go together; after all we have been married 74 years now. It would be a huge adjustment". Siman knew he should let her think aloud and so made no comment. Louise let out a long gentle sigh which seemed a mix of thoughtfulness, sorrow and resolution.

"It's odd, but I would like the satisfaction of seeing my Robert die well and peacefully. I would then have cared for him to the very end ... or should I say to the very beginning. Either way we won't be apart for long".

She placed her wrinkled character-filled hand over Siman's. "Thank you".

Io cycled in to the Fish earlier than normal so as to avoid George, and because she had a mid-afternoon appointment. She had much on her mind as she determined what action to take over the gCow. The sab spoke through the grommets in her ear. "Io dear, it's Mum here. I thought I might catch you before you set out for work ... Greatpa Robert had a fall last night".

She told of the night's events. "Don't worry your-self dear. I'm just keeping you in the picture and will let you know if there is any change. He will be heavily sedated after the operation so there is no point in visiting".

So much in her head, but the bronchs were good for thinking. Oxygen kept her brain alert; she could cycle to avoid others, and had already avoided George. So Io began to analyse her position using the new found energy and passion mined at Monkton Farleigh. Every-thing appeared to shout for equal attention but as she replayed her mother's conversation she agreed that there was no point in visiting. It was Friday; Arthor and Clairu would be in Brighton for the weekend, so she could park Robert's fall at the back of her mind until Sunday evening.

Io found herself in a quandary over George; on the one hand he had provided the listening ear that enabled her to articulate a need for purpose, on the other hand he wasn't going to be someone who could change things. He was trapped in a security institution, a growth industry if there ever was one.

Something had happened the night she saw Daisy the gCow; a raw determination to make a difference had grown within her. George had been an important catalyst for all this but their relationship could only go so far. How could she maintain friendship and make clear its limitations without at the same time hurting George?

She had grown very fond of him. They had talked deeply, especially about each others families. But she couldn't really talk this quandary over with anyone, neither could she fly out to a tropical moonlit pool like the one where she first became conscious of George watching her.

The grommets conveyed a familiar voice. "Could I pick you up for a meal this evening Io?", asked George. He had decided that it was time to develop their relationship further, but she suddenly felt crowded by him.

"Sorry to miss you; I've had to go in early. I'd love to George but not tonight. I've got a lot on my mind because Greatpa Robert has had a fall and I need some space to think". She thought honesty the best course.

"Oh Io, I'm so sorry to hear about Greatpa; he's such ... such a gentleman. You could think aloud with me! You've told me about finding purpose, about your family, about you. Why not chat over a meal?" He was hurt, and it showed in his voice.

Surely men were the ones to disappear into their cave alone, and Io certainly wasn't a man. The comely maiden was sensitive to his feelings but new-found energy pushed her on.

"Don't worry George. I value our friendship greatly, but I've always had moments when I need to be alone. Don't forget that the first time you saw me I was alone with my thoughts as I swam in the moonlight".

"Don't you worry Io, I'll never forget that night!" He hoped it was love more than friendship, and felt reassured when Io spoke. "On Sunday night I'll get in touch so we can fix a time for a good chat. Would you like to cook one of your wok dishes? I'm passing Hiss Farm so will finish now. See you soon".

She had a weekend ahead of her beginning with

Pamela and Gustav, however for now it was the well-worn creative routines of Inflow that would fill her head.

Gustav wondered if he was making his time too accessible. Two more people had asked to see him. However each of the conversations so far had intrigued him. The pod, as he liked to call them, had merely put his philosophy into action. Something disturbed them, in this case Daisy the gCow, and triggered good reflective discipline. They had analysed well using his V2L tool and reached a true conclusion; it was so satisfying after all he had taught them. Then Silvanus had appeared wanting off-the-wall stuff about rider controls; if he was such a whizkid why couldn't he work it out for himself? Why so private? The two conversations side by side had rattled him.

And so it was that with a mixture of curiosity and growing concern that Gustav welcomed Pamela and her godmother Io. They wanted to see him in private too! Perhaps Pamela was being bullied as the only girl in the pod. He didn't think it likely so expected that a few words about distinguishing between teasing and bullying would suffice. And yet?

Pamela had asked Io to lead the conversation. "Coffee?" asked Gustav. "I know Pamela has a taste for straightforward plain coffee that has not been played about with unduly!"

"Yes, thanks. Milk, no sugar please. Just like Pamela". A natural pause gave Io the chance to look around Gustav's study, den, call it what you will. The shelves contained an amazing mix; ancient books, notepads, artefacts, pebbles, a rusty old spike that once anchored down a piece of track on some long redundant railway line.   All appeared to have order.   Steaming mugs appeared.

"I know that Pamela's pod came to see you about a genetically modified cow, if you can call it that.   I'm aware that you are busy and am sorry to trouble you again about the same subject".

"Your help last time was fantastic.   I had never appreciated the power of your V2L idea ..."   Pamela hesitated, not wishing to be disrespectful.

"Go on", encouraged Gustav, looking into her blue eyes.

"Well, I'm not sure how to put it.   It's just that ... it seems that's where the story ends".

And now a passion took over as her body quivered with a mix of anger and excitement.   "Having analysed Daisy we just leave her there!"

Gustav thought a while.   It was a characteristic Pamela had come to appreciate but Io felt very uncomfortable and pulled her legs up under her chair.   Pamela reached out and held her hand briefly; they glanced at each other.   Facial signals put Io at ease.   You could imagine Gustav drawing on a pipe.   He scratched the whiskers underneath his chin.

"Acting might well cost her her life.   After all she is now so totally dependent on the 'caring machine' that she couldn't survive without it.   Also ..."

This time he paused not quite certain how to put it, for the thought challenged him too.   "I don't see my role as putting things into action so much as giving others ideas which will lead to action".

"Isn't that a cop out Gustav?" burst in Io, surprised by the strength of the spirit within her.

"Sorry, I put that too strongly. What I mean is ..."

Gustav interrupted, "No. It's entirely logical. There is only one of me but there may eventually be hundreds of thousands that might take action from ideas I've helped them to discover".

The conversation which had its genesis in philosophical thought nudged forwards towards action.

"Do you know anything about a just war?" asked Gustav as he appeared to throw in a complete tangent. "Saving Daisy would be a kind of war. It should only be begun if it is justified. After all, how many conventional wars have been started on weak grounds only for the attackers to lose face and withdraw after some face-saving stunt?"

Pamela and Io were convinced that saving the likes of Daisy was justified, but they didn't like the idea that she would have to die. Perhaps the caring machine could be kept going until her 'natural' unnatural life came to an end. They left Gustav conscious of more work to be done. His final words rang in their ears and they were more than happy to conform with his request.

"I think this is too important to be a private matter. The pod should all be involved. But there are very serious implications. The powers that created Daisy will not take kindly to being undermined".

The thought slithered through Io's mind that these powers would need another power to challenge them. It was important to propagate the Value to Living index widely; how? Everybody had to become more V2L conscious. It had taken years to get the world to be energy efficient using sustainable sources; the task of realizing ethical efficiency was enormous.

Pamela stayed at Waterbeach Metaguild and Io cycled thoughtfully, slowly back towards Ely and home. The light had just begun to change to evening hues, but it would be several hours before it was dark, hours of great change.

17 Zigzag

What about the risk of being misunderstood? Do nothing, achieve nothing! Red bush tea was made on autopilot. Mind was in a whirl as passion, opportunity, insight, and distant mooing writhed around her head. For some reason she kept coming back to the thought that the disgustingly rude Silvanus might be a key.

Her home in Ely had a good view of the lantern windows perched precariously on the cathedral roof; Io needed a lantern to guide her and tame the powerful spirit within her as she sought to challenge injustice. She could sit beneath it and pray, not for anything in particular but to discover something. Or ...

Over the years Io had found a number of 'thinking places'. The one she had in mind now was to one side of a zigzag path down the slope of a chalk cliff face. It had once been used by smugglers who certainly would have deserved any reward in carrying contraband up such inclines. The cliff was steep but quite safe. The ledge to one side of the path overlooked the sea and was hidden from view.

Quite suddenly she made up her mind. Mum and Dad were away in Brighton, so she could go down to Dorset and work out how to find the power to change things. And this thought surprised, excited, and disturbed her; she would take Silvanus with her. It seemed crazy; he might be working on rider upgrades all weekend; he might think she was after a physical relationship ... but he might also be key.

Before she would never have dared to ring him

but now did so on the off-chance. He was putting his beloved dogs in their kennels for the night and his first thought was that the idiots in the Lakenheath Rider Servicing Complex ought to sort out their own problems. He was intrigued to see it was Io calling.

"Sorry to disturb you but I could do with some advice". There was a pause while Silvanus thought carefully. Was he being setup? Was this a trap? Had someone discovered his cell? He had better respond naturally.

"That's fine. What's the problem?" Silvanus was nervous but tried to speak slowly keeping his tone low and relaxed. Io felt strangely confident; her cause had emboldened her.

"It's complicated and will take some time to explain. You're in the world of mass communication and understand rider technology; I'm wanting to communicate widely and not just through my beaches. Could we meet?"

"Ok. When? Where?" Silvanus sensed that the stale warm air of early summer was on the move; curtains fluttered and lifted his spirit. He was excited that Io needed him, and hoped she answered now and at hers. He couldn't believe her reply!

For a moment time stood still. It was as if they circled one another. It was odd, for subconsciously they both knew they needed each other but had yet to find out why. Could it be that Io's new found purpose was the cause Silvanus needed to take him outside his own self-centred world? Could his ruthlessness be of value to a woman wanting to make a difference? Whatever it was they were attracted by need.

"Could you pick me up from here without the dogs? I'm sure Ashley would keep an eye on them for the weekend. I want you to drive me to Dorset to help me understand what is going on in my head". How come she was organizing him? This cool calculating Io was new to him.

Questions bombarded her mind too. What did Silvanus actually do? Why did Ashley so resent his father? What was going on behind those eyebrows? With George it was a case of 'what you see is what you get'. He was genuine enough and good company but there was little depth. Silvanus on the other hand seemed to have layer upon layer under his control.

"Well, yes ... but I hardly know you. The weekend you say; where would we stay? What would we do?" It must be a trap. He needed to think. Dare he talk? What were her motives? The curtains moved again.

As it happened Silvanus had no work commitments over the weekend. He had pencilled in a walk with the dogs from Cromer Pier south along the cliffs. Instead by late evening he found himself heading southwest in the company of the beautiful and intriguing Io. By 8.00pm he had made all the arrangements, packed to include walking boots as instructed, and headed down the A11. Turning right after Red Lodge through Fordham and the A142 he had made good time to Io's Ely home.

They travelled down the A10 to the M45, set the autopilot for Ringwood and sat back for a chat. Traffic was light and so eCar pods were travelling at 110mph. The weather was clear with good pick up from the strips laid into the road surface; the battery would be fully charged when changing from M27 to A31 after passing Southampton. They had an hour and a half to talk over their sudden engagement in each other's lives.

Talking was easy for they found their thinking mutually challenging and liberating. Initially caution constrained topics, but a rapport and trust built; however Silvanus was blunt in his questioning. "How do I know that I have not been set up? After all you have the high security clearance needed to work on the inside of the Fish while I merely maintain riders".

Io wondered exactly what 'maintaining' meant and was direct in her reply. Conversation flowed, and like a stream between two banks gradually widened. The stream meandered around their family lives; Silvanus was sorry to hear of Greatpa Robert Smith's fall, and Io learned more of why Ashley found his father somehow distant. She asked how Jeanette, Fern, and Ernest were doing; Silvanus told of the two year old twins' tantrums but said that he liked to see a bit of spirit too. Io compared the flat Fenland with the gentle hills of Dorset, the Cromer cliffs with the White Nothe and Durdle Door; soon the warning sounded from the autopilot.

Silvanus drove west along the A31, and then south at the county town of Dorchester along the road that cut through the chalk Ridgeway to expose the vista of Weymouth Bay. Io pointed out the beam sweeping across from Portland Bill Lighthouse and the laser display over Weymouth beach. She let them into her parent's home in Brunel Drive.

They raided the fridge for supper and agreed to turn in for an early night so they could make a good start the next day. It was a moonlit scene when street-lamps extinguished themselves at midnight, but by then both of them had been asleep for an hour.

The alarm went off at six and Io made tea, took some to Silvanus, "Do you like porridge?" He did but hadn't eaten any for years. "Should be ready in about 20 minutes. Have you everything you need?"

By seven they were walking along Puddledock Lane, and then the White Horse cycle and footpath to Osmington, down to the Mills and east along the coast. At the top of the first rise they stopped for a cup of tea. Silvanus disappeared into the bushes for a pee. Io commented that her family called it 'turning your bike' and he laughed out loud. All these moments eased the tension between them and pulled them closer to each other.

As they walked the surface layers of caution began to peel away but they both closely guarded the secrets which they longed to share. They climbed the slippery coastal footpath up to St Catherine's Chapel at Holworth and paused for a while outside looking out over the sea. They didn't go in because Io didn't feel ready to share what the place meant to her. All she said was, "Some time ago I said a prayer in the chapel and I believe it was answered".

Silvanus made no comment. He wasn't as fit as Io and was quite glad to use the break to recover his breath. But they were soon off again cutting across a field towards some coastguard cottages at the top of White Nothe Cliff. He turned to her when they paused by the marker to the zigzag path. "You look very

109

thoughtful".

Io was annoyed by the comment. She thought her emotions were locked away. Perhaps as she neared her thinking place on the cliff she had relaxed her guard, or perhaps Silvanus had a craftiness that could read her mind. Either way she found herself talking about the endless junk that flowed in vast quantities through the Fish. What a fantastic waste so much of it was, a mindless flow.

Silvanus was interested. He wanted to interrupt the 'mindless flow' so that others would acknowledge him for the person he was. His burning passion was a refusal to let the world batter him into the shape of a convenient cog in its huge mechanism. No! He was a person not a thing! Perhaps this Io could help him make his ideas fly.

Their conversations were very different to their first meeting in the Waterbeach Metaguild. There he had invaded her space as she studied a picture. Now it was as if they had known each other for years but had only just started to talk about things that mattered. They had another tea from the flask as the sun warmed them. What a view; it was still, the sea like glass. You could hear the gulls and a distant fishing boat. Io still kept off the subject of Daisy the gCow, and Silvanus avoided talking about rider sabotage, and yet they talked deeply with real conviction until suddenly Silvanus stopped.

He had noticed a smartly dressed country gent approaching; was it him? He talked of how tasty the hobnob biscuit was and that the tea had kept well in the thermos flask. Io was about to laugh at him but caught the warning in his eyes; something serious was going on, so she commented about the sea and casually greeted the gent. Silvanus then relaxed and chatted easily to him about the Smugglers' Path. Soon the man had wandered off and Io asked, "What was that all about? You seemed freaked by him".

Silvanus spoke of a gentleman in smart tweeds who told him off when walking the dogs in Thetford forest. "I thought it might be him spying on me. I have to be careful in my line of work ... even in Dorset!"

Now both of them had been caught off guard. They talked about the incident. Silvanus said it was the gent's self-righteous manner that rankled with him and admitted that it got under his skin but wasn't quite sure why. Perhaps it was his rather patronizing tone. Anyway, they gave him the nickname Tweedy.

Both relaxed some more. Silvanus asked why the dogs weren't welcome in Dorset.

"You'll see. I was thinking about their safety ... and ours", she teased. Now it was her turn. "What do you actually do?"

"I think we need to take one step back and check we have a clear understanding before I answer that", he replied with an easy but more serious tone.

"I'd like that because I've been thinking exactly the same".

They carefully rehearsed their formal positions on confidentiality, communication security, and the regular checks that often scrutinised them; both were used to holding their guard. The checks were as commonplace as going through an airport. She was on the inside of the Fish's secure environment while he was on the outside. As a contractor overhauling riders he needed to know what units to replace and how to upgrade software, but details of the software or anything else to do with rider communication paths were strictly outside his 'need to know'. If they talked much more the security boundary between them would be breached.

"We're nearly there now". Io had led Silvanus down the first couple of zigzags in the cliff face and then diverted off towards what looked like a sheer drop to the sea below. For a moment his mind checked his relaxed state, not because of the height but because of questions it raised about Io. Was she a decoy? Was she just doing her job? Why here?

They reached a ledge, quite snug and completely out of sight to all except fishing boats in the bay. Silvanus thought one deft push from Io and he would be in the sea. And yet she drew trust from his suspicious heart. "I need places like this to think, and I don't reckon the dogs would have made it. It makes me feel insignificant and yet loved by our Creator; the sea is always the same and yet with so many moods. It can shout and froth, or be still and reflect as a mirror; but the tides never slow. The earth's moon has power over any storm".

Over the years Io, named after a moon herself, had found many storms abate here. In her angry adolescent years she had first discovered the place, and since then the genetic and nurtured inheritance from Greatma Louise Smith had brought her to this cliff ledge.

Their conversation had cleared the decks. On the 'thinking ledge' they talked more freely. She told him of Daisy and how passionately she wanted to change the world. Ashley had told his father all about V2L so Silvanus understood Io's passion. In turn he shared his anger at being treated just like a useful cog in some vast machine.

"If you think Daisy is some kind of cow-queen in an appalling milk-hive then I feel like a worker-bee in a communications-hive".

Io looked out to sea. She had been right to take the risk with Silvanus. She turned and looked directly at him.

"Do you realise that we basically share the same cause? Yours is about people taking you seriously; mine is about people taking created beings seriously".

Unusually for him he encouraged someone else to speak. "Yes, go on". In his imagination he was looking down at the two of them like a pair of birds in a nest. Could this be a partnership of passions?

"Well, what would happen if we shared causes?" Io had crafted her point carefully before asking. A fire burned within her. "As a human you are the peak of creation; if we could get the world to take Daisy's life seriously then I believe it would take you seriously too".

There was one mug of tea left in the thermos; they shared it. Silvanus was deep in thought. Could she be right? Could his cause be caught up in something greater? Without realising it until now he saw that he had been self-centred, almost like that wretched Tweedy. He would need a little more time to think. His spirit soared as if flying out across the sea.

He felt suddenly fulfilled, and cooed to himself.

18 Cracking codes

"It's been right under our noses. The Even Space Protocol, or ESP, is open-source so anyone is free to build and operate riders. All they have to agree is that they will keep an equal distance from their neighbours. The rider network is constantly adjusting depending on how many thousands are up there". Silvanus was in his snug at the Five with just Charles. Goodness knows what the weather was doing outside. It was early summer.

They had entered at different times, joined in banter at the bar, enjoyed pork scratchings, and then Silvanus slipped away to the gents. In the corner cubicle, so rarely used, was a panel which opened if the toilet roll holder was turned through a right angle clockwise and back again. Then Silvanus' mechanism of white corridors and doors, which were set differently each time, disorientated guests until they finally entered his secret snug. He had set it all up for Charles to follow in a few minutes.

"What we have to do is generate virtual riders operated from the one we hijack so the others all 'think' they have many new neighbours and gradually disperse. That will slow information flow until someone takes notice. Can you do that?"

Charles had an amazing gift; he could see codes like many can sightread complex music. He intuitively knew the shape, pattern and rhythm of seemingly pointless packets of information. "Shouldn't be a problem if it's open-source. How many virtuals would you want and how should the number grow?"

They discussed various options and decided gradual changes would be best. That way Inflow would pick up that information transmission was slowing down, check to see rider density was good, and inform authorities that something was amiss. If the information flow decreased beyond a certain point less important transmissions would be closed down. Silvanus still wanted to broadcast his demands to the world, so he would make sure the right channels stayed open.

Lakenheath Rider Servicing Complex maintained around three hundred machines, and there were similar facilities in southern Germany, Portugal, three in Russia, with another five in America. That meant around three thousand riders covered the northern hemisphere. To make an impact on such a dense network would require considerable numbers of virtual riders. Charles saw no problem; if you could make one you could replicate as many as you needed.

"We will have to survive extreme cold and heat depending on the time of day; we need our own oxygen and food supplies. The module is already adapted for a maximum of three days, so if we start as soon as we are at full altitude on the first night we should generate three hundred or so over a couple of hours". Silvanus had calculated all this some time ago.

The conversation lasted for an hour and a half as Charles' quick technical mind mapped out the problem and probed Silvanus' scheme. He loved these challenges; the adrenaline would keep him going for hours. Silvanus would not be surprised if Charles worked all night to present him in the morning with the solution to using the ESP for hijack of European communications which would have an impact across the world. The Spaniel loved a good bone to chew on.

They didn't meet until after lunch the following day. After all, gaining a reputation at their local pub for drinking too much too soon might draw attention to Silvanus' hidden snug. True enough Charles grinned, childlike, through his bleary-eyed face. The code was cracked and virtual riders could be created in any number and at any or varying frequency. As usual he had further questions.

"Why do we have to be up there? I haven't got a head for heights! And how do we get down? If we fly the rider everyone will know where we are".

Silvanus was cautious because Charles was a sponge and absorbed endless detail, and like a sponge he was not watertight. Too much information would be a security risk. If he burbled on about codes and the like few would take notice of his eccentricity, but if he knew about their escape method from the rider it would be unwise and Silvanus would never get him up there in the first place!

Nicknames have an uncanny power or a subtle deftness to uncover traits in their named-one. Charles the Spaniel loved to chew on a bone but could be distracted by chocolate! Silvanus explained that the two of them needed to be on board so they could hijack earthed sourced control flights without being hijacked themselves. And now for the 'chocolate!'

"What would you like for the first meal when we're up there, and do you want to take a camera to capture the dawn?" Two pieces were always better than one.

Meanwhile the pod was cracking a code of conduct. Alfred had found a curt summary of six 'just war' conditions. Sphinx had been rather enthusiastic about who was the custodian of the conditions and how many there were. Zoid had gone a step further to produce three criteria as to the conduct of war; these were relatively new as the International Criminal Court was only established in 2002 by the Rome Statute. Pamela acted as convener but the group knew each others' foibles so well that conversation flowed naturally and purposefully.

Would the cause of liberating Daisy and her clones be for a 'just cause'? All agreed that their V2L evaluation overwhelmingly proved so. Even allowing for significant errors of judgement her score was well below others. So far so good; the first condition was met.

Now the second condition, 'war must be lawfully declared by a lawful authority', was going to be tricky. Who would represent Daisy's cause? Why not them? Over and over they had heard the United Nations' mantra 'for every right there is a responsibility'. Its mission statement also included the phrase 'speaking truth to power'. That's exactly what they should do. They were the 'lawful authority' but how were they going to declare the war for Daisy?

Alfred took them to the third point, 'the intention behind the war must be good'.

"How's that different to being for a just cause?" asked Ashley.

"I suppose", ventured Will, "that the first point is

general and the third more specific. So, for example, encouraging democratic government might be a just cause, but regime change could be unacceptable". It didn't take them long to agree that a future free of gCows was a good intention.

The next condition on Alfred's list, 'other ways of resolving the problem should have been tried first', threw up further debate. Now their emotions bonded them together and focussed minds through the lens of youthful passion.

"If Daisy's existence is secret how can we get her story out in the open? We could broadcast Pamela's video, but how?" queried Ashley. He had many quest-ions but something deep within warmed him to the cause; it was excitement that they might actually make a difference in the world. Surprisingly his father Silvanus came to mind and he wondered why. Metaguild wasn't just about thinking straight, it was also about action. His young heart beat faster.

"We're going to need some help from others on this one". Pamela's wisdom proved apt.

The final two on Alfred's list, 'a reasonable chance of success', and 'a means in proportion to the end' would depend on the method used. Here they were completely stuck, so they went for a walk to see if they could find Gustav. He met them with his usual interest but was beginning to feel drained by being the connection between so many separate conversations.

As once before he drew Susan into the mix. It was summer and she was toddling around dead-heading her roses. She agreed with the pod that the just war conditions had a part to play but asked what weapons would be used in the gCow war. There would be considerable vested interest involved. The machinery which 'cared for' the gCow clones hadn't come cheap for a start, and presumably the production was economically very efficient. Methane from her waste would power the equipment, and the milk produced would be of high quality. Her sponsors could be the government or multinational venture capital, and either would be hard nuts to crack. It could take years.

The pod were in awe and respect of Susan as her hologram spoke gently to them. The roses being pruned in the background only enhanced her comfortable wisdom. She ended with a question, "How long do you think it took women to get the vote in this country?" It put their enthusiasm into perspective once they had found the answer through sphinx.

Gustav suggested they kept the conversation going but that finding practical ways forward would not be easy, and would have to be part of the discussion as to whether it was just or not.

19 Not a moment

For years he had been building literally and metaphorically for this moment. The cell would be triggered. Gradually members found their way in as he controlled the ever-changing white path of doors and corridors. Sometimes they would walk in almost directly and other times it was like being lost in a maze. There was often a look of surprise and relief as the final door opened into his snug. How was it that locals didn't notice Silvanus' group disappearing into the gents? Simple really, and the best ways of defeating security have to be simple, because the gents was on the way out to the car park at the back of the Five; locals thought they were going home.

Inside, Silvanus had a real sense of urgency. Charles and Io had completed the jigsaw in his mind. Charles had cracked ESP which was the last practical piece in his sophisticated and yet clean plan. The module in which he and Charles would live had been tried out several months before. Silvanus had connected it to his snug so that unawares Charles could try it out. He had sat down in his usual chair even though it was in a different section. Silvanus had placed a few personal effects on the table so Charles felt at home; in fact he was so absorbed by something in his overactive mind that he hadn't really noticed the changed environment.

All well and good, yet the jigsaw had been incomplete. Yes, all the practical pieces were in place but the jigsaw had somehow lacked focus and purpose. The satisfaction of an integrated simple plan with everything dovetailing beautifully wasn't enough. Io was the key. Liberating gCows gave a higher purpose, but it was Io that made the connection. She appeared so innocent but to her credit had enticed Silvanus and drawn him into her plan; no, their plan. She would never in a million years have known how to hijack a rider.

Each member of Silvanus' Cell was told that his or her particular task was now to be initiated. Some of them were quite simple but all included a challenge. Victor was of similar height and build to Silvanus but had gone bald years before. Now he had a wig which was a reasonable match for Silvanus' full head of hair. He had Silvanus' walking clothes and was to make all seem normal at home. The dogs would have regular walks in Thetford Forest. Silvanus gave him a few final details.

"Victor, take these Fishermen's Friends and if a gent in tweeds with neatly trimmed beard makes some fatuous comment about the dogs just breath all over him and feign a lost voice. And for God's sake always keep the hounds on their leads".

Jeanette had to call at the pub as usual and tell them the lads were away on some stag do. She was very happy to booze her way through a few days.

"Don't overdo it now. I also want you to listen carefully for anything unusual in their reactions. Remember to keep a simple log in this fancy little paper notebook". Jeanette loved to doodle in pencil. Her tasks fitted her perfectly.

Montague's task was the most challenging. He had gained his pilots' license many years ago while employed to fly along power lines so that monitoring equipment could check for hot-spots in cable joints, or signs of wear in tower structures after heavy floods or snow. The latter meant flying in strong crosswinds because that's when the towers were most stressed. Montague could fly easily in any conditions. He'd done a bit of crop spraying too and felt liberated when airborne. But his challenge would stretch his skills to the limit; the rig had been fitted and successfully deployed a dozen times.

The cell drew so much energy from Silvanus when he was on a high. His purpose, whatever it was, gave them purpose; and they knew that when it was all over he would let them into his plans. My word, they had had some adventures!

"Ok. Off we go. There's not a moment to lose".

It was Ashley's turn to be with Silvanus, so arrangements needed to be put into place to explain why Victor would be keeping an eye on things. This was a small change to Silvanus' original plan but had been brought on because, after his conversations with Io, Silvanus had felt in his bones that acting sooner rather than later was vital. Everything had been due to kick in the following weekend when Ashley would have been with his mother Holly but he had brought things forward.

Much was changing in Silvanus. He was embarking on a very dangerous mission. Riders were not built for manned flight, so performance of his module was a matter of life and death. Getting back would be full of danger too ... what if he didn't make it; he hadn't recorded or written anything for Ashley.

He had just discovered a new perspective which

now included others not just himself. It was time to tell Ashley what was going on, and he had another important appointment with the twins. They went for a walk without the dogs.

"Ashley", he began, the full name indicating a serious topic. "There's something you need to know".

"Yes, father ... there always is". He sighed because he was tired of hearing yet more of Silvanus' latest plans. There was always some scheme or another; Ashley wasn't interested any more. He missed the dogs.

"Hear me out. This is different. It's about your Daisy". It was like a light switch going on; Ashley was listening now. Was this another manipulative ploy?

"How do you know about Daisy?"

"I've been talking with Pamela's godmother". Silvanus kept it a little formal because he didn't want his son to pick up on how much Io already meant to him. Within careful boundaries, and compelling Ashley to keep things highly confidential, Silvanus explained that he was about to hijack the rider network to force the world to acknowledge V2L and stop manufacturing gCows.

"It's very dangerous, Ash. I might not come back. I just wanted you to know why". There was a lump in both their throats.

"Dad". They hugged so tight and tears flowed. They walked on. Tweedy passed by but said nothing. Silvanus hardly noticed.

"There's something else you need to know, Ash. I've never told you why your mother and I parted company. If something were to happen I'd want you to know how hard I tried to make it work". Ashley listened carefully; his father had never talked like this before.

"When I met Holly I thought her physically quite stunning; you know, with high cheek bones and a complexion that required no additions from plastic surgery or make-up. But I found out that her personality was flawed by an insatiable appetite for attention. I've never thought myself a weak man, but my energy was constantly eroded by Holly".

The son wondered why his father, his Dad, hadn't told him before! Years of misunderstanding and hurt might have been avoided. Even if he now had the bridge he had so long craved there was so much traffic it needed to carry. Ashley wanted the chance to have those conversations; what if Dad never came back? The young lad whispered a prayer of utter desperation.

"O God, if you're there please, please bring Dad back home".

Silvanus continued, "I tried everything to understand Mum but after ten years of marriage I gave up and handed control over to cynicism. I loved Holly but found her impossible to live with and no longer tried to have real conversation, and so I gave up on a living marriage. We lived inside a beautiful shell, but a virtually empty shell. I was determined that Holly shouldn't destroy me. I evolved an internal mechanism to remove emotion and involvement from the equation. Whenever I spoke I anticipated early interruption and therefore would score my sentences in terms of completed time compared to full time. 50% was a good result. Occasionally she would listen and we could talk deeply, but it was too rare.

Generally speaking this mechanism worked well

but I could not come to terms with her pessimism. Everything was about to fail, she always saw the worst in situations. Occasionally, although God knows I tried, my way of coping would break down. Then she had extraordinary power to change me from a mature strong man into jelly. She used the cutting edge of her tongue and she could make me reject any sexual desire by so patronising me that I no longer cared. I became less than a man, and inside there burned a fury tempered only by my love for her. What other husband would put up with such voluntary torture? It had to come to an end".

20 Dying

Robert knew his time was near and he looked forward to the journey he alone could make. He felt so tired, and so loved. What would it be like to be free from his ancient wornout body? What would it feel like to be free from time's remorseless pace? You could move forwards and backwards, sideways, up and down, but you couldn't shift from your slot in time.

He had said all he wanted to those around him. What a fantastic family; he was truly blest, for every one of them had come to say goodbye. It had all been so natural, sad at times but put into perspective by the adventures of his life and theirs. He had wasted little on trivia, and the rat-race had not tricked him; play hard, work hard were his themes. He felt amazingly fulfilled and had the honesty to be justly proud and so grateful to the Good Lord for the gift of life.

Right now though, he wanted to be alone. They would understand, and might even be relieved. The funeral or celebration had a rough shape to it; his favourite piece of music would be played loud, however little was definite. He had often said that it would of course be about him but it was for them, so they should craft it. The signal was raising his right arm. Summoning all his strength he just managed it. They kissed him gently and left. Louise was last and gave his hand a long squeeze.

Once they had all gone Robert relaxed and whispered a simple prayer to the all-hearing One, "Thank you". He let his breathing slow down and then decided it was time to never take another breath ... and he didn't.

The scan of his femur had made it clear that the head had crumbled off rather than broken. His ancient frame had lost strength so that the fall created a multiple fracture. Replacing the joint would not be practical. There was a family conference with Janu in the driving seat. She included everybody in the decision about her father's care, and especially made sure he could express his views. Robert would never walk again and had relied more and more on his 'electric quad bike' as he called it.

"I don't want any more fuss. I'd like to die at home with Louise nearby. I know you'll look after her. We won't be apart that long". He had winked at her and she had smiled. "There is one other thing, and I hope you don't misunderstand. I'd like to die alone please".

Arrangements had been made. Robert was made comfortable in his bed overlooking the pier. It seemed as if his vigour might return, however it soon became clear that he was waiting ... waiting for ultimate freedom.

St Paul's was nearly full. All the virtual seats were taken and many of Robert and Louise's friends joined in from their homes. The vicar knew them well and was spot on. She maintained a delightful balance between dignity, sorrow, humour, creativity, the familiar and ... Robert's choice of music. A well-constructed account had been written by Arthor; it drew from snippets given to him by family members. The vicar made it live, and paused long enough for laughter, sighs, hands to be held. She simply closed with "Thank God for Robert's life, and through him the life of so many here. In the name of the Father, and of the Son, and of the Holy Spirit". She sat down and for a moment or two there was quiet.

Many decades before, a rather inadequate band played to a rather inadequate audience in a rather ordinary pub. They described themselves as the Sultans of Swing. Mark Knopfler took the title and crafted a powerful successful piece which needs to be played live rather than in the tame atmosphere (or lack of it) of a recording studio. This was Robert's choice; its vital spirit grew slowly towards a climax of electric energy as high notes vied for attention. Then it relaxed as the rhythm returned. Somehow what started life in a pub now expressed something of Robert's spirit. There were tears of sorrow, joy, vitality, strong emotions mixing; there were no tears of regret. The family knew Robert had lived and died well, and that they should be proud of the part they had played.

To one side of the church was an area where a glass wall gave excellent views; sound was relayed inwards but noise from within was contained. Silvanus had asked if he could bring the two year old twins, warning that they might be as good as gold or have wild tantrums. Io warmly welcomed his support and showed him the room. "Make yourself at home. As soon as the service has ended I'll pop back and we can go to the reception. Just now I want and should be with my family".

When she returned Fern and Ernest were playing with toys and didn't notice her entrance. Silvanus was embarrassed; Io was not. He had been crying.

"That was amazing. I wish I had met him. I didn't realise you could choose music like that in church. Even the twins had been absorbed; looking around somehow aware that caught up in Robert's life was a much bigger story. I'm sorry ... it got to me. I haven't cried like that since I first realised I could no longer live with Holly".

Io said nothing. She smiled an understanding which put Silvanus at ease and drew him closer to her; what a remarkable woman. They encouraged the twins to pack away the toys; it all seemed so ordinary and yet a flutter ruffled Silvanus' spirit and bore it up to a higher more noble plane.

21 Riding

The rider was nearly ready. She tugged on eight hemp lines which tethered her to the dock. The scene was dominated by the matt black titanium disc. Helium now filled her huge tanks; the final software transfer for new Inflow modules was making good progress. She would lift that night. All seemed well.

Charles and Silvanus had been on board for some time. Some crafty design work meant that one of the processing bays was empty. All the computing, transmission and reception gear had been fitted into the other five bays. The two men's living quarters were cramped but since they had evaded detection so far they were unlikely to be discovered now.

The wind was kind so that Inflow control set a gentle take off to save fuel and therefore prolong the time she could be floating. It took three hours to reach the full altitude when Silvanus asked Charles to begin deployment of virtual riders.

Soon the ESP protocol was confused by an additional 350 'riders' slowly appearing one by one over northern Europe. The existing neighbours moved away so that a large hole appeared in the rider cover. Communication slowed as signals were routed over longer paths, and earthbound transmitters found their signals weakened. Satnavs packed up, some less important shopping television channels disappeared ... and Inflow noticed the change. Even Jeanette's favourite soap packed in for a while!

"What the hell's going on?" barked a burly voice

down the secure ground line from his home to Inflow control.

"I don't know, Sir. I've never seen anything like it. We've had far more than the usual number of successful rider launches during the night, and yet comms has rapidly deteriorated when it should have grown more robust. We've never had that many riders over Northern Europe before".

"Put out a security 'high alert' status and call up 'hacker-crackers' to find out what's happening! It might be a cyber-attack".

"Yes Sir!" Everyone followed the emergency protocols but a sense of fear and anxiety pervaded. They spoke in a slightly higher than usual pitch.

"I'll get in touch with European colleagues to see why they think so many riders have been launched".

Silvanus had hacked into the secure ground line and knew that his interference had been noticed. All to plan so far. He asked Charles to begin reducing the number of 'virtual riders' so that communications would return to normal. This move was also noticed; it reinforced the unease at Inflow.

Government had been in formal contact with Inflow too. Tomorrow night was election night; millions would be watching. It was vital that no glitches interfered with democracy. "Our people are looking into it. In the meantime, Sir, we have brought about a rapid improvement". He hated not being in control. The better signals were not of his doing. Silvanus rubbed his hands with glee. In the cramped module secreted into the rider they enjoyed a celebratory bar of chocolate with caramel flecks, the Spaniel's favourite.

"Charles, now that we've let them have good signals again are you ready for our broadcasts? We'll go for the 9.30pm advert breaks and the 10.00pm news".

"Do you want to go straight to all channels or just a few to start with as we designed?" asked Charles. He loved the power wielded by his ever-busy brain; at last he was being taken seriously. In the pub Jeanette noted that her soap returned but was frustrated to have missed so large a chunk of storyline. Her notebook began to fill with scribble. Adverts were due shortly.

"Oh my God! What's that?" Her cry alerted regulars to the screen where a short video clip accurately describing Daisy's plight appeared. In just 40 seconds V2L had been shown to be the way forward. The clips were anonymous except for Daisy. Silvanus had a rare gift for angle and had edited Pamela's video well; the sadness in the gCow eyes, the deep natural yet unnatural breathing, the pipe work; it hit home. The closing comment. "Sorry to interrupt but we thought you should know", led back to normal transmission.

The 10.00pm news clip was not a repeat. It worked at two levels; if you hadn't seen the first Daisy clip all necessary detail was there; if you had seen it the message hardened and this time the closing question was "Shouldn't you vote for those who will make a difference?"

He wasn't dressed in tweeds now but the meticulous beard twitched anxiously. "Tell me more about your observations. We need anything different that might link to this rider network hijack". It was clear by the tone that national security were extremely concerned about events.

"Well Sir, it was quite clear that I rattled Silvanus Woodlander who is a lead contractor at Lakenheath. I think underneath he's a very angry young man. The only time he didn't rise to my quips was when he was with his son. Io Smith, who we've been watching for some time, is of concern. George Freeman is our main operative and, as you would expect, we've been keeping an eye on him too. He has regular conversation with Smith but nothing much has come up. There are some puzzles too because two days ago Woodlander attended a Smith family funeral".

"Ok, where is Silvanus Woodlander now? Contractors serving riders are bound to be a weak link". Again the intense manner showed in Tweedy's interrogation.

"He was at home with his son Ashley who seemed normal to me and answered the door. His father was coughing Fishermen's Friends everywhere". But something in his bones made Tweedy uneasy; something was different ... but what?

Inflow was like a hive responding to an assault. High emotion did not lead to clear analysis but adrenaline spurred on questions about possible weakness in security. So rarely nowadays were breaches made at obvious points in this chess game; it was those who could move a humble pawn behind the enemy lines that were more powerful than the multi-talented rooks. Rather like nuclear power stations which operated on full load, day after boring day, there was a buzz when something changed.

"If this challenge to our rider network is not eliminated it poses the greatest threat to our national security (and international standing) I can think of in all my years experience. You have my authority to get him, or her, or them. Clearly better alive so we can find out all they know, but dead if there is a chance of them repeating this". The Prime Minister had convened COBRA and was preparing to give a press conference ready for all the breakfast bulletins. Funny how it was still called a 'press' conference when presses hadn't been used for decades.

Ivana Spicer was new money grafted onto old. Her father had made his money exploiting the weak democracy of Russia by extracting vast revenues from oil and gas reserves. He had the usual trappings of wealth: a pet football club, an oversized yacht, and fancy homes here and there. He spoiled himself but had never spoilt his daughter; she had had to work her way up through the business. As she did so she had become more and more disillusioned.

A glamour holiday to Nepal has opened her eyes. Life expectation was far too low with basic services and infrastructure amazingly unreliable. There was no oil in Nepal, only vast mountains – which is why she went. Everyone seemed happy to climb a mountain, leave their detritus behind, exploit the delightful indigenous Nepalese, and then head for the next entertainment. She had read Edmund Hillary's biography; the friendship he struck up with Sherpa Tenzing lead to a passion to improve the lot of Nepal. Climbing Everest was a passion, improving Everest's home nation was a greater one.

Ivana had learnt to take time out. She would make it clear that certain blocks of quality time could not be interrupted unless there was an absolute emergency. Everything was diverted to her team, which thrived on the challenge. One evening as she sat watching the flames dance like angels over the logs of an open fire an ember flew out onto her expensive rug; before she could get to it a hole had been burnt and the rug ruined. She was annoyed, yet only a few months previously she had compared the wealth of her father's company with that of Nepal. It could effectively buy the beautiful nation several times over, and that became a deeply uncomfortable thought. A small hole in a rug didn't really matter.

To cut a long story short disillusion gave birth to conviction. Ivana entered politics and soon her passion became that of others too. She rose through the ranks whilst having a reputation for both conviction and honesty. This was often to her disadvantage with party officials but not with the electorate.

But she needed a spark to set alight the campaign in its dying day ... and she like everyone else had seen Daisy. That's it! Ivana made arrangements.

22 Backing

Throughout the next day Silvanus had made small changes to the rider network which operated normally enough but still made it clear to Inflow that the cyber-attack was continuing. The rider he had hijacked worked perfectly. He and Charles turned in for the night ready to monitor breakfast bulletins.

What a fantastic political contrast appeared; at last the election excited people! The prime minister did his Churchillian piece to camera and made it clear how dangerous was the game the hijack terrorists played. And then Ivana offered to take up Daisy's cause and argue the V2L at international level. Silvanus couldn't believe it; his heart raced and he sighed for Io.

What should he do next? If he were to slow the network again it would only annoy people (including Jeanette and the locals). Could he modify the Daisy clip to urge people to vote for Ivana; it would show them he knew what was going on and that they could make a difference. Silvanus worked away with Charles to modify Daisy video version 2 into an upbeat and very short Daisy version 3 congratulating Ivana on her principled stand and including an invitation to support her which seemingly came from Daisy's lips. He was quite pleased with the result and set it up for the evening news and main advertising slots.

After some more chocolate Charles and Silvanus turned in; it had been a long yet most satisfying day. In the early hours they would escape from the rider leaving it in place and covering their tracks. They were positioned far above the North Sea several miles off the Norfolk coast. The theory was simple; first their temporary home would be jettisoned with them still inside to shelter them from the cold as it fell at speeds up to 800 mph, and then protect them against friction heat as the atmosphere thickened. At two miles above sea level they would open the door and freefall using their arms and legs to steer them away from their temporary home which would plummet into the North Sea and sink beyond trace.

This was all very well but, because Charles didn't have a head for heights, Silvanus hadn't bothered to explain the plan. He thought it wise just to tell him what to do when the time came. All went well as the rider shed the capsule. Charles would leave it first and freefall until half a mile above sea level when his parachute would automatically open. Silvanus would follow but open his chute earlier so as to be well above Charles.

But Charles refused to go through the door. The whole escape plan could be jeopardised with module and occupants heading for the sea bed. No amount of logic would persuade him. In the end there was no option. Silvanus operated the chip in Charles' neck which paralysed his body; his grip failed and he fell out of the module, but because he couldn't use his arms and legs he stayed too close and eddy currents trapped him in its wake and spun him round in all directions.

Montague was ready, his catching net deployed below one wing which had a leading edge of razor sharp steel. Just like the old Post Office trains of yesteryear he would catch Charles in the net, simultaneously cutting the parachute traces. On his infrared screen he could see the module but no Charles. At last Charles' parachute opened but because he had been spinning wildly some traces jammed. The jolt on his paralysed body wasn't noticed because he had passed out with fright.

Montague used all his skills, diving to line up with Charles. There was an enormous lurch as the blade cut through the parachute traces, all except one. The plane was pulled to one side Montague yawed from side to side to cut through the final rope, then the plane was free, but Charles was also free. Falling, falling hopelessly headlong to the grey water below.

There was no way Montague could have caught him, and anyway he was on the lookout for his son. Silvanus' parachute was quite majestic, an easy catch. This time the wing blade cut through all traces and, just as in the many practices, the plane hardly noticed its extra load. Silvanus scrambled on board, jettisoned the net and closed the door.

"Where's Charles?" he shouted; Montague didn't answer.

23 Loose ends

They raised their glasses to toast the success of the mission. One pint remained in front of an empty chair. Jeanette placed a packet of pork scratchings beside it. "He loved his scratchings", she burst into tears. Silvanus put an arm around her shoulders but his thoughts were elsewhere.

The funeral was a minimal affair because nobody in Silvanus' cell reported Charles' disappearance. Two days after the incident his body had been washed up on the shore by a gas distribution station near Mundesley on the Norfolk coast, but nobody had come forward to identify him.

Inflow put two and two together and reckoned the incident might have something to do with rider cyber-attack but could never pin anything on Charles. It looked like suicide with all the parachute traces cut. Silvanus had to admit that it was his fault Charles had died, but he also had to admit it was all rather convenient. He now had the perfect alibi.

Ivana Spicer romped home with a thumping majority, and true to her word her first use of political power was to launch a Royal Inquiry into gCow production, include V2L on the national education curriculum, and apply to the United Nations for an opportunity to give a speech in New York. Time would tell if these first signs led to real change.

It was a chilly summer's morning with a strong east wind coming across the North Sea. She was later than expected and had been walking, jogging and walking to arrive unflustered but with glowing cheeks. Her coat was open and flapping in the wind. He was hopping from one foot to another trying to keep warm at the Old Lighthouse on the cliffs east of Cromer. "Sorry to be late. There was some panic at the Fish and I had to send off a report from home before I could drive over".

"Oh, don't worry, but I'm freezing and need to walk to find my feet again". Almost without realising what she was doing Io unbuttoned his coat and hugged him tight so that her heat could pass to him. Silvanus responded in kind as he hugged her, surprised and delighted. She was innocent like a dove; his heart fluttered. After half a minute Io broke away, and broke the silence.

"Come on, I'll race you to that tree". She was off. Little cheat, thought Silvanus, I'll teach you; but she was fitter by far and waited for him. Perhaps she wasn't quite so innocent after all. "Warm now?" she asked, laughing.

They walked along the cliff for half a mile before cutting south ease across a golf course to St Martin's Church at Overstrand which had clear glass windows. Io suggested they had a look inside and had arranged for it to be open; Silvanus thought it very appropriate because Charles' death weighed heavy on his mind. In front of a picture of a guardian angel they lit a candle for the Spaniel; Io said a moving prayer giving thanks for his life, and the potential liberation of gCows. She seemed respectful but strangely upbeat. They discovered an historical link to both Africa and the abolition of slavery.

140

After a while they explored the tower, where they came across two identical bags. Io suggested they investigate and Silvanus pulled off a cover to reveal a Brompton folding bike; she kissed him lightly on the cheek. "I wanted to thank you with something a bit different, something for your true health".

Silvanus hugged her deeply. "I don't know what to say ... Thank you. Thank you. Thank you". Io showed him how to unfold his bike and soon they were off along the lanes through Sidestrand, Trimingham, and up to beacon hill. Later they would cycle through Mundesley, hide the bikes and walk along the coast past the gas distribution site where Charles' body had been found.

But now they found a place overlooked only by the sea and snuggled up like two magnets drawn to each other. There was so much to talk about. Ashley was transformed from being ashamed of Silvanus to having a deep and sustained pride in what his father, his Dad, had achieved. The dogs were pleased to see their boss home and so was Io.

They were soulmates.

... and then ...

2

future

Loose Ends

Here's to
making better
decisions for future
generations. England
could be an example
across the world
in the 2060s.

01 Undrunk

English drizzle screened the trawler from view. It was another tedious day but a mug of coffee in the wheelhouse warmed Skipper's hands while his crewmate tidied up the deck ready to haul in the net.

"What the hell was that?" shouted both men in unison as coffee spilt over the wheel and blood spilt from a nasty cut to a forehead. Instinctively the engines had been shut down as the trawler lurched in the swell. Silvanus' rider module had just been found two years after Charles' body was washed ashore.

His death had been a very convenient alibi for Silvanus Woodlander and the successful rider hijack, which had held northern European information to ransom; but he missed Charles Jarman, his faithful Spaniel. The first anniversary had been poignant as he and Io had cycled on their Bromptons along the coast where the bloated body had been found. It was bright sunshine but a shadow hung over his heart.

Somehow the second anniversary had been worse; this time a pint of his favourite bitter stood undrunk at the head of a table in the Five Miles from Anywhere hostelry. There was no Jarman to drain the jar of ale. Grief was utterly hollow and ached. How uncanny then that on that very evening local channels should tell of the trawler's discovery. Silvanus tightened; might he be discovered too?

Forensics linked the module to riders, and hence to Inflow security. The remains of a chocolate bar wrapper bore sufficient DNA to link the module with the late Mr Jarman and the sample taken from his body before cremation. No other DNA was present because Silvanus had been very careful. Module discovery was a possibility in his rider hijack planning. Security personnel were puzzled because it seemed possible that the module could have borne two people.

Tweedy was put on the case. His terrier instinct was ruthless. The identity of the deceased had been on public release but he kept back the fact that Charles' pic had been modified. In fact, as far as he knew, he was the only one with that information; yes, the scan result was buried in a general database but if you weren't looking it was a needle in a haystack.

After the successful hijack both Ashley Woodland and his father Silvanus wanted a fresh start. They spent more quality time together and Silvanus began to impart some of his engineering intuition to his firstborn. The lad learned fast and had soon constructed an electric go-cart from various scrap parts found in his father's garage.

Life for Silvanus had become complex when it came to female companions, each of whom held a bond of affection for so very different reasons.

His estranged wife Holly was Ashley's mother and the new energy between father and son also warmed the relationship between parents. Neither would want to reverse time and live together again but both wanted friendship to mature.

Jeannette Pack had the role of girlfriend, however she was now 33 and although still of catwalking capacity had lost some of the freshness of her youth. The demands of their twins Fern and Ernest, now happily at school, did not leave her much energy or space to enjoy anything apart from her beloved soaps. She was not the sharpest tool in the box, but Silvanus was fond of her and sought to broaden her horizons.

Io Smith was the third woman in his life. They were soulmates. He wanted to settle down with her in his Eriswell Cottage but she kept a certain distance while encouraging the conversation between their spirits. He was her Serpent; she was his Dove. Together they had proved a powerful combination which had briefly controlled northern European communications.

All three women wished to mark Silvanus' thirtieth birthday because they felt he had at last come of age as a person. He had found a cause and discovered others besides himself. But how? Who should take the lead?

Ashley Woodlander and William Inchbald had both come of age by celebrating a joint eighteenth birthday on a date exactly between their actual birthdays. They had invited a wide range of friends made at Waterbeach Metaguild, all of whom were off to different universities or apprenticeships across Europe. It had been a slightly zany occasion, with in-house jokes, and had been based at the Sports Entirety Gym and 'Clubhouse'. A set of different challenges, some sporting most not, had pitted Ashley's team against Wills'.

It was all very good humoured with parents acting as stewards, umpires, referees etc. Ash and Will gave a combined speech, each reading alternate paragraphs. They warmly and genuinely thanked their respective parents, but added a few stories to mock their efforts and keep them in perspective.

Ashley wanted to do something for his father, his Dad. The unknown quantity had been Io; she had turned up at little notice and swept Silvanus off his feet, not in the sense of a whirlwind romance but by making a deep connection with the ground of his being. It was at the same time as he had deeply connected with his father. Were the two changes linked in some way?

Ashley decided to talk to Pamela Smith who was there when they discovered the gCow factory in Monkton Farleigh Mine. Io was godmother to Pamela and it was a good relationship.

"Pamela, I'm not quite sure where to begin but, can you help me understand women!?" he asked with a chuckle.

"I'll do my best but they are a bit of a mystery to me too, even though I'm on the inside!" Pamela's strong blue eyes looked at him through her glasses and twinkled with the delight of banter; she held her head slightly to one side and asked, "What do you want to know?"

"Dad has three women in his life; they are all special to him in their different ways. It's his thirtieth birthday in October and they want to celebrate it but nobody seems to want to take the lead."

"I'm not sure you should be asking about women," responded Pamela. "It's about you! Why don't you organise something?" Her bright eyes looked straight into his. I'd be happy to help."

"Brilliant! Why couldn't I think of that? You're so wise." Ashley gave her a peck on the cheek. "Thanks."

He went on to discuss with Pamela how he viewed his father's women. Holly would always be Mum and, although she could be controlling, as he matured their relationship had evolved robustly. Jeannette was different, not in terms of conversation even if somewhat shallow but because Silvanus wanted to keep her as a girlfriend. Yes, he supported their twins but Jeannette somehow always felt like an extra.

Io was different. Ashley could see how much she had done to liberate Dad from himself. She might even have been instrumental in restoring the bond between estranged father and son. Ashley always thought his father looked like a bull mastiff dog, rather ugly but somehow attractively so. Silvanus could appear aggressive and belligerent, and he certainly had been, but now the softer features of his face had became more marked. Ashley was drawn to Io and wished that she was his godmother, not just Pamela's. She seemed to complete the female role models that he needed. He felt comfortable with her but couldn't yet see how things would develop. Time would tell.

He took up Pamela's offer to help with Silvanus' birthday and decided he would organise everybody. It would need to be a bit different.